JOSIE

CATHERINE TRIMBY

YOUCAXTON PUBLICATIONS
OXFORD & SHREWSBURY

Chapter 1

A WOMAN SCREAMED. The noise faded, leaving an echo reverberating eerily through the van. Before the echo had been completely subsumed by the engine's diesel roar, the voice rose again and became a long, high-pitched cry of desperation and despair.

There was silence for some minutes. No one came.

Banging and frenzied kicking shattered the short silence. Then another cry, low this time, like an animal caught in a snare; helpless and hopeless.

Josie shivered but not from cold, though she was cold. She huddled in the tiny space; she was unable to stand up, unable to turn round and unable to respond to the person screaming. Her own profound misery now compounded by someone else's even greater agony.

She was frightened. She didn't know why. The screaming woman posed no immediate threat. But Josie couldn't think logically any more. She had no control over her own situation. She felt like a ragdoll, dropped by a thoughtless child into a torrent of swirling brown floodwater spiralling uncontrollably down a drain. She was spinning helplessly through an underground culvert, not knowing if the current would carelessly offer escape via a distant pinprick of light or if she would be sucked down into the muddy depths and ultimately be washed up as detritus on the river bank.

It seemed hours later when the van shuddered to a halt. There were lights outside but Josie couldn't see anything other than a neon glow through the tiny tinted window above her head. She had no idea of the time as her watch had been taken from her. She knew it must be late in the evening. Thankfully the crying had eventually subsided to occasional moans and sobs. The banging petered out, too, perhaps through exhaustion. She didn't know; she didn't want to know. Now, as she waited in the confined space for someone to come, her fear returned and her shivering intensified; her teeth chattered and she wrapped her arms around herself, more as protection than for warmth. There were shouts outside and the clank of keys unlocking doors. She heard a key inserted into her door. It was opened and she was yanked by the arm out of the cubicle and pulled to her feet. Handcuffs were snapped shut round her wrists. Chains and keys jangled discordantly.

'Come on, hurry up.'

A short, stocky, uniformed woman hustled her to the steps at the front of the van. It was a huge relief to be out of the cramped cubicle. Josie stumbled down the steps, her legs unco-ordinated after being constricted for so long. She nearly fell but the woman put an arm around her and not unkindly helped her to regain her balance. The cold November night air slapped Josie hard in the face and she was aware of the inadequacy of her clothes. Rough hands manoeuvred her through swing doors into a low, shed-like building where several men, also uniformed, sat behind desks with files and papers piled around them. Bare light bulbs hung from the ceiling casting a harsh light. Her handcuffs were removed.

The swing doors were opened again behind her and Josie saw another hand-cuffed woman being pushed into the shed. She was younger than Josie, maybe early twenties.

Her mousy hair was long and untidily scrunched into a ponytail. She looked as frightened as Josie felt. Her face was white but her eyes were puffy and red. Josie thought she must have been the person screaming in the van and for a moment felt a pang of compassion. The feeling didn't last; she didn't have the energy to care about anyone other than herself and, anyway, the first man was asking her name and she had to concentrate.

'Welcome to Edgehill Prison,' he said without a trace of irony, as he started to fill in the first of many forms.

There was a clock on the wall above his head and wearily Josie registered the time. It was 10.50 p.m.

It was nearly midnight when Josie and the other woman were led by two officers, a man and a woman, along a concrete path that ran between several low Nissan huts. It had been raining heavily and there were puddles on the path. Josie sploshed through the water and felt it permeating her thin shoes, rapidly making her feet cold and wet. She and the other woman had their arms full of bedding: each had a duvet, a sheet, a pillowcase, a towel, also a pack of toiletries and several plastic bags, one with a packet of cereal and a carton of long-life milk in it. They trudged dejectedly after the officers to a single-storey, brick-built building. The male officer unlocked the outside door with a key from the chain attached to his belt. He pushed it open. It was quiet. There were doors on either side of a long, grimy corridor that seemed to stretch forever in the dim light.

'Toilets here and showers here,' he said, indicating rooms on either side of the passage. He strode further on.

'You're in here.' He turned to Josie, shoving a key into the keyhole of a door with a lopsided number 18 attached

3

to it. He took a felt-tip pen from his pocket and wrote her name on a scruffy board beside the door. It had obviously had many names on it over the years and as the pen didn't work very well her name was more or less illegible.

'What's your number?'

'I can't remember.'

He sighed and peered at a piece of paper that the female officer produced from her pocket then wrote AT119360A on the board underneath the name Josephine Anderson.

'You'll have to remember in future,' he snapped, obviously tired and clearly longing to get back to the warmth of the reception area.

'And you're in 19 next door,' he said to the other girl. He put a key in the lock of the adjoining room and filled in her board too: Joyce Davies AT263011A.

'You'll hear the tannoy in the morning. Listen out for it telling you where to report for induction at 9.30. Don't be late. Oh, if you use the showers take your keys with you and lock your rooms while you're out.'

With that both officers turned and disappeared down the passage into the cold, wet night leaving the two women staring hopelessly after them, unsure what to do next.

Josie hesitated, looking for guidance from Joyce, but quickly realised that was pointless. She entered her room and dumped her bedding onto a wooden bed that had a thin mattress on it. Wearily she started to make the bed then became aware that Joyce was now standing in her doorway tears pouring down her cheeks. She was shaking uncontrollably.

'I don't know what to do. I want me Mam.' Her voice rose alarmingly.

Before Josie could respond someone shouted at them from the room across the passage.

'Shut up, for fuck's sake. Who the hell d'yer think yer are, wakin' everyone up?'

Josie, now mute with fear, backed further into her room gesturing to Joyce to leave.

'See you in the morning.' She managed to whisper, horrified at the outburst from the unknown person.

She had never used obscene language and rarely even heard it except on television. She shut and locked her door and found herself trembling again. Joyce was still crying forlornly outside in the passage, the sound becoming muffled as she also went into her own room and shut the door, quickly locking it. Both doors clicked shut imprisoning the women still further in their own isolation. Somehow Josie managed to put the duvet cover onto the duvet and the pillow case onto the thin, dirty pillow. She was exhausted and the effort needed to make the bed was almost too much; it was tempting just to fall onto the bed with her clothes on, but she desisted. She rummaged in one of the bags and found her pyjamas and also her watch. There was no curtain on the little window and she turned the light out to undress, terrified that there might be someone lurking outside in the dark who could see her.

Her pyjamas offered the only comfort of the entire day. They were warm brushed cotton and smelled of her washing powder from home. She slid under the duvet into the cold bed, hugged herself tightly and, sobbing softly, tried to sleep.

It was still dark when Josie awoke after a restless and disturbed night. There had been noises throughout; she didn't know what had been going on. Now she was aware of two women arguing loudly outside her door. The row seemingly was over a broken hairdryer, one woman accusing the other of dropping and breaking it. The language used shocked Josie again and a sense of intense desolation shrouded her like an impenetrable mist. She had no idea how she would cope. She tried to see the time on her watch but had to turn the light on to do so. She crossed the room and flicked it on then immediately off in case someone was outside and could see her. Her watch said 7.15 a.m. She needed the bathroom but was too scared to leave her room. She slid back into the warmth of her bed and wondered what to do. The women arguing in the passage finally moved away.

Ten minutes later Josie knew she had to pluck up courage and brave the corridor. She couldn't find her dressing gown so decided to put on her trousers and warm jersey rather than walk down the passage in her pyjamas. Carrying her towel and wash things she very cautiously unlocked her door as quietly as she could. The passage was empty though there were sounds of radios and televisions coming from many of the other rooms. Josie scuttled to the end of the passage, trying to remember where the showers and toilets were and hoping she could get there and lock herself in before anyone saw her. She could hear water running and then a loo flushing but luckily one cubicle was free so she dived in and locked the door. The water was hot and comforting. She decided against washing her hair but had a good shower and felt a bit better. When she came out there was a large black woman cleaning her teeth at one of the basins. She had a blue towel wrapped like a turban round her head. She rinsed her mouth and spat as she turned to look at Josie.

'Hi, yer new?' She dried her face with a small towel.

'Yes' Josie clutched her wash things closely to her as a barrier against some unknown fear.

'What's yer name?'

'Josephine Anderson.'

'Josephine Anderson.' The other woman said the name slowly. 'Where 're yer from, Josephine Anderson?'

'Near the Welsh border.' Josie didn't elaborate.

'Well that's nice then. I'm Michelle and I'm the house rep. Yer can ask me stuff if yer don' know what to do. I'm in room 12, on the left.'

She smiled at Josie, showing more gold teeth than Josie had ever seen before. However, she didn't seem unfriendly.

Josie hurried back to her room remembering that she had been given a packet of cereal and some milk the night before. There was a plastic bowl and spoon in the polythene bag with the rest of her meagre possessions. She ate her cereal slowly; it was tasteless. She was too scared to see if there was anywhere to make a cup of tea, which she would have loved. Her last proper meal had been lunchtime yesterday.

The tannoy speaker was situated on the wall outside her room and she was initially startled by the loudness of the frequent messages that were being broadcast. Women were being called to go here and there and to do this and that, none of which made any sense to Josie. It was disorientating.

As she finished her cereal Josie looked properly at her little room. Her relief at having her own room was enormous. She had expected to have to share and the thought of living with a stranger had been daunting. The room contained a cupboard with space to hang clothes and with drawers underneath; there were a couple of shelves fitted to the wall and a battered easy chair in the corner by a small square table on which was perched an ancient-looking television set. There was a small washbasin. The room was drab, but it wasn't unacceptably dirty, she decided. She rubbed her sleeve on the misted-up square of window and looked out. Through the gloom of a dreary November morning she saw another similar building at right angles to hers with scrubby trees and shrubs, a few desolate leaves clinging grimly to the branches, planted between the two buildings. There were figures scurrying along the paths, wrapped in coats, heads down, going somewhere, she had no idea where. She turned away from the grimy window; her first priority was to find some sort of curtain. Being spied on from outside terrified her.

She pondered the problem. She unlocked her door and, taking her key with her after relocking it, she moved cautiously down the passage to room 12 and knocked timidly.

'Yeah?'

Tentatively Josie opened the door a little way.

'Sorry to interrupt but I wondered if you knew where I could find something to make a curtain?' Her voice sounded squeaky with apprehension.

Michelle was sitting on her bed smoking and watching breakfast television. She seemed barely to register Josie's presence, but with her free hand she rummaged round under her bed and brought out several scruffy pieces of material.

'Here yer go.' She thrust them at Josie. 'One of them might do, they're old bits from other rooms. What yer don' want, bring back.' She turned again to the television. 'Oh,' she said without turning round, 'they're goin' to put new ones up, any time soon, I think. Others weren't fire retardant, see, so they was scrapped after the last girl left.'

'Oh, thanks.'

Josie tried not to breathe; the air in Michelle's room was thick with smoke; the material in her hands stank as well. Not wanting to show her disgust and holding the material as far from her as she could, without seeming too rude, she quickly left the room and returned to her own.

Joyce was now standing outside her own door looking bleary and unwashed. She was in her pyjamas and clutching her coat round her shoulders.

'I don't know what to do,' she moaned. Her hair, greasy and lank, half-covered her face.

Josie was irritated. She wanted to put her makeshift curtain up.

'You'd best get washed and dressed. Down there.' She pointed towards the showers.

Joyce looked so woebegone that Josie relented slightly.

'You can come into my room to eat your cereal if you want.' She paused. 'Have you got a curtain?'

Joyce shook her head.

Josie indicated the pieces of material she was still carrying.

'You can have one of these to put up, but get dressed first.'

Joyce looked as if the whole idea of washing, dressing and eating breakfast was far too difficult to think about, let alone execute.

Chapter 2

THE DISTANT SOUNDS of 'Three Little Maids from School', banged out on a tinny piano, permeated the small room at the back of the village hall. Josie was wedged into an upright chair behind a table piled with costumes, an old Singer sewing machine just visible in front of her. She was trying to mend a large rip in a bright orange kimono. Her mouth was full of pins and she was rummaging in a box of cottons attempting to find one that wasn't too much of a mismatch with the material.

Members of the cast had continually interrupted her, wanting clothes that she had mended or leaving costumes that needed altering. She didn't feel as if she was making any progress and the pile of costumes didn't seem to be diminishing. It would be the dress rehearsal tomorrow, Sunday, and time was running out. The Northwood Amateur Operatic Society was about to open its annual July production with *The Mikado*. It was a seriously important event with passions and tempers running high. The singer playing Katisha had a sore throat, the producer's wife was in hospital and the painting of the scenery wasn't finished. However, by comparison with other departments, the wardrobe room was relatively peaceful and well organised, though Josie didn't think it was. She liked things to be just so and the jumble of costumes and piles of material strewn over the table and floor felt like chaos.

Dress rehearsals were always a nightmare in her admittedly slight experience. She took the pins out of her mouth, threaded the machine with orange thread and tried to draw the kimono's fabric together. She thought about the size of the lady who would wear it and wished there could be a super-rapid diet enforced, otherwise she expected to have to re-sew the whole thing again after the first night. Possibly even after the dress rehearsal.

It was nearly two years since Josie's Dad had encouraged her to join the operatic society, which he had long supported.

'We need more sopranos,' he had said. 'You can sing a bit, you'd enjoy it and we can go together. It would be fun.'

She wasn't sure, but she had capitulated as she wanted to please him. She knew he was relying on her to drive him to the weekly practices.

To her surprise she rather enjoyed it. She found she didn't mind standing in the back row of the sopranos and miming when she didn't feel comfortable with the high notes; she found she liked the actual singing but she also found out that acting wasn't her thing. She had hated being singled out or asked to do something solo, she had wanted to curl up and die. When she had said she wouldn't take part in the annual show there had been surprise from the producer and, she sensed, criticism from the other girls in the chorus at her unsociability, so offering to help with the costumes seemed a reasonable compromise. Now, as she struggled with the ghastly orange kimono she wasn't sure it had been such a good idea after all. Maybe performing would have been the easier option.

She was hanging the offending garment on the rack with the other completed alterations when the door opened again and a man came in. He was in the chorus and she knew his name was Mike. He was clutching a dressing gown round himself rather ineffectively with one hand and carrying a guard's tunic with the other.

'Hi there, Josie,' he said breezily. 'Can you let this out for me?' He thrust the black tunic at her.

She was surprised that he knew her name; she didn't think they had ever spoken before. She took the tunic and looked at the seams on the inside.

'There's not much spare material.' She glanced up at him.

'I'm sure you can squeeze another inch for me.' He rubbed his rather large stomach and the dressing gown sagged further open, to Josie's discomfort. He only had a pair of boxer shorts on. He noted her expression but just grinned at her.

She wondered if he was pulling her leg. The seams really had nothing to let out and anyway the garment looked big enough.

He moved closer to Josie, too close for her liking and she backed away but found herself hemmed in by her own chair. He leaned over her; his breath was on her cheek. She could smell beer.

'I'll see what I can do in the morning.' Back off, she thought.

'Don't you want me to put it on so that you can see what needs doing?' He was running his eyes over her which made her feel even more uncomfortable. 'It would be easier to pin it like that, wouldn't it?' He started to strip off his dressing gown.

'I don't think that's necessary,' she said hastily, not liking the sight of his bare torso. 'Can you write your name on a label and stick it on, please?' She passed him a roll of labels and a pen, hoping he wouldn't argue.

He pulled his dressing gown back on and shoved her tape measure, pins and scissors out of the way to make a space on the table. He bent over to write, glancing at her as he finished and making great play of unnecessarily licking the label before sticking it on the tunic.

'There you are.' He handed it to her with a flourish.

Josie sensed he was playing with her. She took the garment from him and folded it up before putting it on the pile of costumes that she still had to alter.

He winked at her. 'See you in the morning, then.'

He went out, whistling a phrase from 'The Flowers that Bloom in the Spring'.

Josie picked up the tunic and looked at the label. 'Mike W' was written on it in capital letters. It was presumptuous of him to assume she knew his surname. She thought it might be Williams but she wasn't sure. Worse, though, was the way he had looked at her. Men didn't usually look at her the way Mike had just done and she had no idea how to deal with it. She was certain now that he had never spoken to her before but she had noticed him in the chorus and was aware that he was often the centre of attention. What did he want? She found herself wishing that Di, the official costume mistress, had been here instead of driving to fetch her son from a scout camp on the Welsh coast. At least she should be back in the morning, hopefully before Mike returned for his costume. She could deal with him.

Josie sat down again and started on another alteration.

Chapter 3

MIKE LOOKED AT HIMSELF in his bathroom mirror the following morning. It was quite difficult to see his face satisfactorily as the mirror was splashed with so much dirty water and smeared with gel, 'Sea Salt' hair spray and toothpaste spittle, that the available space for reflection was minimal. He plastered some more gel onto his hair and half turned to see the effect from the side and back. He decided it looked okay.

Today was the dress rehearsal. He wasn't looking forward to it. There were too many tiresome old men telling him what to do and frowning at him if he made a joke. Most of the women were rather po-faced as well. Being in the operatic society hadn't turned out how he had thought it would. He had only joined for a laugh when someone in the King's Arms had said they were short of tenors and that there were lots of girls on the pull. He knew he could sing quite well and the silly old producer had said so after his audition when he had belted out a couple of karaoke numbers. Joining had been a doddle. The expected female talent hadn't materialised, however; everyone was either married or spoken for, except, as far as he knew, Josie. He would do the show this week then chuck it in. Learning all those stupid songs had been quite hard work.

Meantime he needed a bit of a distraction, which was where the silly little Josie came into the frame. She was rather pretty in a dowdy sort of way; probably a bit older than him, but she had a surprisingly good figure and her legs weren't bad either. She seemed a complete innocent and it would be fun to see if he could get her back to the flat before the week was out.

Yesterday afternoon had been a promising warm-up, he decided. Seeing how the land lay and all that. Actually, he was quite pleased with Josie's reaction to his chat-up line. He had certainly rattled her cage. He reckoned she was a little prude, but could easily be manipulated when he turned the real charm on. Today would be round two. He liked a challenge. She was probably asking for it; they usually were.

Chapter 4

JOSIE SLOWLY FINISHED HER BREAKFAST. On Sundays she had a boiled egg just as she had all through her childhood. She liked routine. She was sitting at the kitchen table looking out onto a small but tidy back garden and there were fields beyond. In the summer there were usually sheep grazing peacefully. The house had been her parents' home; she had been brought up here, gone to school locally and then to college not far away. She had never lived anywhere else and nor did she want to. Her parents had married late and she was their only child. She suspected that giving birth had been a disagreeable experience for her mother. It wasn't talked about but she had been led to believe that her mother's real or imagined ill health stemmed from a difficult labour. She wondered if her mother had resented her. It was true her father had spoilt her. He had often said she was she was his 'little girl'.

Her mother had died when Josie was twenty-two. The doctor had said it was her heart but Josie wasn't sure. When there was ironing or housework to be done her mother had regularly pleaded chest pains and fatigue, but she seemed to have enough energy for shopping and treats. It was usually Josie's father who did the chores.

'I'll do it, Josie girl,' he would say 'You've got your project to finish' or 'you've had a long day at college. I've been sitting around doing nothing.'

More often than not she had let him do the work on his own. Sometimes they would wash up together and he was always pleased to have her company.

'We're a famous team, Josie girl. We'll have this done in no time, you'll see, and then we can watch *Strictly*. Your mother wants an early night.'

Josie was just finishing at college when her mother died. She had been thinking of leaving the area and getting a job further south. Whether that would have happened she wasn't sure now. What she did know was that she had felt her mother to be unreasonable in dying at that particular moment because it meant that her Dad now needed her to stay at home and help him. He had suffered a few 'bad turns' and the doctor had told him to stop driving.

'You're my little chauffeur,' he used to say when they returned from a shopping trip on a Saturday afternoon. 'We make a great team, Josie, you doing the shopping and cooking and I can just about manage the garden. We'll get by, you'll see.'

She felt she couldn't let him down. It seemed right to put off the idea of moving away, just for a few months anyway, until he could manage on his own. But of course he didn't manage on his own and the months stretched into years and now it was ten years later and she was still at home. She had found a job with the local council in the planning department. It was a boring job but steady; a bit like me, she thought, with rare self-appraisal, but it suited her well. Life had become routine. It was predictable and secure. Their social life was intertwined: weekend shopping together, out to the operatic society one night a week, pottering in the garden on a Sunday. That was about all. She had never been interested in social media; she didn't have a Facebook page or use Twitter. Girls at work sometimes teased her about her refusal to live in the twenty-first century but she didn't mind, nor did she mind having no friends of her own age. She laughed at the possibility of boyfriends when her Dad brought the subject up, a bit apprehensively, she remembered.

'You'll want to be getting married soon, Josie girl,' he had said. 'Then you'll have to put your old Dad in a home.'

'No, Dad,' she had responded. 'What would I want to get married for when I've got you to change the fuses and grow the spuds?' She had managed a smile.

He had chuckled, and she knew he was glad she had no plans to move out.

Then her father had also died. That had been totally unexpected. He had a massive heart attack. He was seventy-five and she was thirty-two.

The house was hers, mortgage free, and there were a few thousand pounds in the building society 'for a rainy day', he had always said. She had her salary and a pension in due course. She could manage. There was no reason to change anything. In fact she doubted if she knew how to change anything even if she wanted to. The routine had become completely automatic.

She missed him. It had been difficult to go into his bedroom after he died and see the old photograph of her Mum on the dressing table, the darts tankards on the window sill and his battered radio on the bedside table. She cleared his clothes from the chest of drawers and cupboard and took them to a nearby homeless centre but otherwise she touched nothing. She didn't need the space and there seemed no point in getting rid of the furniture. She did think about moving to somewhere smaller, maybe a flat or a two-bedroom house, but it was convenient where she was and she didn't want to go to all the hassle moving would entail. Probably she wouldn't find anywhere better. It was easier just to carry on as before.

Josie had also carried on going to the operatic society each week. She knew they wouldn't miss her if she stopped but it was a habit and she did like the music. People had been sympathetic when her father died and she had been touched with their concern. It seemed only right to stay and then to help Di with the costumes for the summer show. Now there was only a week to go before they had their August break and she could then decide if she wanted to start again next season. She finished her coffee, cleared the table and started to think about the day ahead.

There was a smell of stage paint as Josie entered the village hall. Two men in overalls were painting a canvas flat on which was drawn the outline of a flowering cherry tree. Josie didn't have much artistic sense but even she could see that the tree bore small resemblance to the sort of cherry trees she had seen in the local park and she hoped the end result would be an improvement. Perhaps Japanese cherry trees weren't like English ones.

Di was already in their little wardrobe room busily sewing a kimono hem when Josie entered. She bit the thread and put the kimono down.

'Hi, Josie, how did you get on yesterday, then?'

'All right, I think, though there is still rather a lot to do, I'm afraid. I expect you've seen.' Josie put her handbag into a drawer and then turned and rummaged in the pile of costumes until she found the black tunic that Mike had left.

'I don't quite know what to do about this.' She held the garment out to Di. 'He wants me to let it out but there isn't any spare in the seams. What should I do?'

Di took it and looked at the label.

'Oh, him.' She raised her eyebrows. 'He's a bit of a menace, always wanting something or other, just for attention, I reckon.' She turned the tunic inside out. 'You could insert some of that blackout material if you think it really necessary, or we could call his bluff and do nothing?'

Josie looked alarmed at the thought of telling Mike she wasn't going to do anything.

'Do it then, if you think we've got time.' Di laughed kindly. 'Otherwise he might badger you, I suppose.'

'The cast haven't been called till 1.30, have they? We've got till then to finish everything?'

'Should be okay if we get a move on. I'll do the rest of the pips and pops on the sashes when I've finished this.'

'Thanks.' Josie sat down on the other side of the table and started to unpick the seam of Mike's tunic with a sharp pair of scissors.

Soon there were sounds filtering through to the wardrobe room of the pianist practising the overture, helped by a somewhat screechy violin and a rather hesitant clarinet. The producer's voice rose above the music and the stage manager's increasingly tetchy responses ensured that the music was ultimately drowned out. Josie and Di carried on sewing, but they were continually interrupted by cast members coming to claim their altered costumes. The excitement of the impending dress rehearsal was growing.

'Bloody prima donnas,' Di growled under her breath as yet another actor flounced out of the room unhappy with the colour, length or fit of their costume.

Then Mike came in.

'Finished it for me, darling?' he oozed charm in Josie's direction.

She handed over the completed tunic, avoiding eye contact.

'You are a sweetie. It'll be perfect.' He barely looked at the tunic before doing a twirl with it held against his chest.

'Thank you so much. You'll come and watch, won't you, to see how marvellous I look?'

Josie glanced up at him, uncertain how to respond.

'You can stand in the wings you know and get a good view from there. I shall be looking out for you. Must dash, got to get the old 5 and 9 slapped on.' He waltzed out winking at her as he left.

'You've obviously made a conquest there,' Di commented dryly as the door closed behind him.

'Not intentionally,' Josie replied looking worried.

'Do you want to watch the show this afternoon?' Di asked as she started to mend a broken fan that the props department had left on the table. 'We'll have to split the week between us so that one of us is on duty for emergencies each night. What do you want to do?'

'You choose. I can do any night.'

'Well,' Di thought for a moment. 'I want to see it with Peter, so maybe we could come on Wednesday to watch. I can be on duty Tuesday and Thursday if that suits you? There'll be the party after the show on Saturday and we don't want to miss that, so we can both be here that evening anyway. Can you do Monday, Wednesday and Friday then?' She cut a piece of Sellotape and wound it round the fan's handle.

Josie said she could and that she would quite like to watch the dress rehearsal that afternoon if Di didn't mind.

'Sorted, then,' Di said cheerfully. 'Now we'd better get this last lot finished pronto or we shall be in everyone's bad books.'

The dress rehearsal was, unsurprisingly, a shambles. Cues were missed, words forgotten, scenery fell down, the prompter lost her place, the men's chorus was singing flat and the producer shouted at everyone. To cap it all the man in charge of lighting managed to fuse all the lights and the stage was plunged into darkness, leaving the three musicians gamely trying to find their way through 'The Sun whose Rays are all Ablaze...' Yum-Yum, whose number it was, flounced off stage announcing that she was never, ever coming back.

Josie, who had abandoned her viewing place in the 'opposite prompt corner' because she kept getting pushed aside by over-enthusiastic chorus members, was watching from a seat as far back as possible in the body of the hall; she found herself giggling helplessly when the lights fused.

'What's so funny, then?'

She felt a hand placed on her thigh. In the darkness she had not seen Mike coming down the side aisle and plonking himself in the chair next to her. She tried to squirm away from his hand but it remained rather too firmly pressed on her thigh, his fingers moving upwards ominously.

'Oh. You startled me. It just seemed funny...' She dried up, not wanting to share the joke and uncomfortable with his proximity. She wished he would take his hand away. She felt violated somehow. 'I really ought to go. I think Di might need me.'

'Don't go, we're just getting comfy, aren't we?' He moved his hand and put his arm round her shoulders instead, pulling her towards him. 'Anyway, Di's having a cup of tea, I saw her in the green room.'

'No, really, there are things I should be doing.' She wriggled free of his arm and got up. In the darkness she half-tripped on the adjacent chair leg. He put out his hand to steady her and grabbed her left buttock, accidentally or not she didn't know. Now, even more embarrassed and uncomfortable, she pulled away again and rushed down the hall just as the stage lights came back on.

'See you for a drink then, after the show tomorrow night.' He called after her. Josie didn't respond but the producer turned round from his chair in the front row. He was clearly near the end of his tether.

'Shut up, for heaven's sake, I can't hear myself think.' He turned back to the stage. 'At last, Sparks, about time too.' Then he turned to the musicians. 'Can we start the number again from the top?'

The pianist played an introduction but Yum-Yum failed to enter.

'Yum-Yum?' the producer screamed in despair.

He's close to a nervous breakdown, Josie thought, as she hurried backstage, eager to keep clear of both him and Mike.

Yum-Yum reappeared and stomped onto the stage muttering fiercely sotto voce. The second act limped on, but Josie decided she would forgo watching, even from the wings. She could have that pleasure on Tuesday night out front, if she wanted. Hopefully a proper performance would be more rewarding than this chaotic dress rehearsal, even if it was unintentionally funny. Mike wouldn't be able to pursue her on Tuesday; he would be in costume and banned from 'front of house'. She had heard his drink invitation but wasn't sure what to do about it. Most of the cast would be in the green room after the show and she wouldn't have to be alone with him if she did go. She would see. Right now she was annoyed with him for sitting beside her without an invitation and she was puzzled. Have I led him on, she wondered, searching for any clue during the last rehearsals that might explain his sudden interest in her. She couldn't think of anything. She certainly had no intention of leading him on. She had hated his groping hands.

Chapter 5

CONTRARY TO EXPECTATIONS there had only been a minor costume malfunction, as Di called it, for Josie to deal with on the first night. She had therefore spent the evening sitting in the wardrobe room with the door open listening to the familiar tunes that were punctuated, rather thrillingly she thought, with applause and cheers from the audience.

It was a full house, made up, inevitably, of friends and family of the cast, so possibly not the most critical audience. It was exciting, though, to hear the first round of applause from the audience after Nanki Poo had sung 'A Wand'ring Minstrel I'. It was surprising, too, that the performance had apparently gone as well as it had, considering the fiasco of the dress rehearsal. The worst thing, seemingly, was when a batten came loose from a backdrop and had to be speedily pulled off by a stage hand, nearly tripping up the Mikado in mid song. It was true, too, that the over-large lady in the orange kimono had split her side seam yet again as she struggled to reach top 'G', resulting in a rapid running repair done by Josie. Nonetheless she found her excitement rising as the evening wore on and by the time the cast had taken their last curtain call she was longing to join in the congratulations and be part of such a successful evening. She was dithering in the passage outside the wardrobe room, trying to find the courage to stay for a drink and wondering what to do about Mike if he appeared, when two of the girls from the chorus came rushing down the passage.

'Come on, Josie!' one of them shouted as they made their way to the green room.

Josie hesitated briefly before following them and finding an ecstatic cast re-living every moment of the supposed triumph. The conversations abounded in superlatives and endearments accompanied by much arm flinging.

Drinks were being liberally downed and egos equally liberally massaged. Most of the cast had failed to remove their over-enthusiastically applied make-up, possibly clinging on to their moment in the spotlight until the last moment, ensuring their other halves would undoubtedly complain about the state of the pillowcase, bathroom basin or shirt collar. Maybe even workmates or office colleague would raise eyebrows in the morning at orange pancake still visible round the hairline.

Josie sidled over to the bar, squeezing through the scrum of bodies and hoping to avoid Mike. She was relieved that she couldn't see him. She planned to have one soft drink (after all, she was driving) and then slip away. Her plan was immediately thwarted by Mike arriving at her elbow, putting an arm round her proprietorially and asking her what she wanted to drink. Josie immediately regretted her decision to enter the green room.

'No, no, its fine, I'll get my own,' she protested, reaching in her bag for her purse at the same time trying to wriggle free of his arm.

He brushed her remark and her hand aside and waved a ten-pound note at the barman. 'One white wine and another lager, please.'

Josie tried to protest again, saying she didn't want alcohol, but he wasn't listening and he shepherded her through the throng to one side of the room where he pressed the wine glass into her hand. His other arm was pinning her to the wall. He breathed into her face.

'That was a great performance, wasn't it? Cheers.' He took a large swig of lager and shifted himself to put his free arm round her shoulder, squeezing her against him.

He was clearly elated and determined to share the triumph with her, blow by blow, not waiting or wanting to hear her opinion. His voice droned on and on, mostly talking about himself.

Josie felt really uncomfortable. She realised that she could either put up with him until she could decently make her escape or risk annoying him by walking away, and she knew she didn't have the guts to take the latter course. His arm remained heavy on her shoulder and she didn't like his beery breath fanning her face. Reluctantly she sipped her wine as she listened to his resumé of the evening. She wondered what the other girls were thinking; she noticed one or two of them watching but she didn't know what their expressions meant. Was it pity or admiration? She was sure they would have had a put-down line to get rid of this sort of unwanted attention. She tried looking everywhere but at his too-close face.

She didn't find him attractive anyway. He was heavily built with quite a large stomach and she didn't like the way he had plastered his dark hair with gel. His eyes were small and his face rather podgy. To make matters worse he was grinning rather knowingly at her and she felt as if he was metaphorically undressing her – not an experience she ever wanted him to have in real life and it was disconcerting. Consequently she found herself drinking her wine rather too quickly just to have something to do rather than have eye contact with him. I'm not used to this, she thought, I wish I had the confidence of other girls who would have got themselves out of this sort of situation without difficulty.

'I'll get you another,' Mike broke off from his monologue. He took her empty glass and turned towards the bar.

'No, no thank you.' She was flustered. 'I must go, I've got an early start tomorrow,' she lied, and free now of his restraining arm she edged towards the door.

'You owe me one, then,' he said. 'Tomorrow night after the show?'

'Maybe, yes, no, I don't know.' She escaped, ran down the passage and fled from the village hall. Her car was nearby in the car park and she drove home carefully, knowing that just the one glass of wine was having an effect on her, or was her confusion the result of Mike's unwanted attentions?

Chapter 6

MIKE CRAWLED OUT OF BED on Tuesday morning. He had stayed rather a long time in the green room and when he was finally kicked out he went with several others to The King's Arms and didn't reach home until the early hours, when he collapsed unwashed into bed. Now his head ached and his mouth felt like sandpaper. He was well accustomed to both sensations.

After several cups of black coffee and some paracetamol he located his briefcase from under the kitchen table, hoped that his day's schedule was still in its folder inside and cautiously made his way to his car, which was parked on the unweeded drive by the front door of his block of flats.

He was a salesman for an agricultural seed merchant and his customers were mainly farmers. The farms were dotted along the border with Wales; some were prosperous but others were impoverished hill farms offering little custom. Most of his money was made on commission, so he was loath to miss a day's work unless he was genuinely ill. He groaned as he realised that today's clients were mostly hill farmers and he could be facing a financially fruitless day.

He felt really awful and in his mind, as he drove, he blamed that silly little bitch for walking out on him last night. The evening had not gone according to plan. If she had been receptive he wouldn't have gone to the pub and got drunk, would he? Should he abort his seduction plan or not? Was she worth it? These weighty matters preoccupied him for the hour's drive to his first client. He knew it was fortunate that the road that morning was fairly empty as his driving was less than proficient. He had nine points on his licence, so was very familiar with the motoring courts and knew that he was likely to be facing disqualification if he wasn't careful.

At his last court hearing a few months ago the chairman of the bench rather pompously announced 'you really must be more careful, Mr Williams. You drive for a living and one more slip-up will mean you are off the road for at least six months. You do realise that your driving on this occasion has fallen well below the standard of a safe and prudent driver, don't you?'

Mike had nodded agreement through clenched teeth and left the dock, several hundred pounds worse off, and with an additional three points on his licence.

By the time he was bumping up the unmetalled farm track towards his first client, cursing the damage to the suspension of his company car, he had decided that he might as well have another go with Josie before abandoning her for someone else. Except that, currently, there wasn't anyone else even vaguely on the horizon. He had rather exhausted the local village talent and would have to trawl further afield if he wanted to find a new target.

What should his strategy be? He pondered this as he drove on to his second appointment after a fruitless call at the first farm. The farmer had been out and his wife wasn't prepared to commit to expenditure in his absence. Mike made another appointment, trying to sound conciliatory but inwardly cursing the wasted journey and only partly blaming himself for not making a follow-up phone call to the farmer yesterday to confirm the appointment. He might have some explaining to do back in the office. Wasted mileage was not viewed favourably.

Half the fun of a conquest, he had long ago decided, was in the chase rather than in the possibility of embarking on a long-term relationship. He certainly enjoyed the fulfilment of his sexual desire but it was so transitory as to be insignificant and no girl to date had become a fixture in his life. It wasn't what he was interested in; a few weeks with one girl, at most, and then he was ready for another conquest. He got bored easily; that and the fickleness of women were his excuses for the inevitable break-ups. He never indulged in self-examination as to why women might not wish to continue a liaison with him. He didn't for a moment consider it to be any fault of his when the relationships failed. Anyway, the thought of settling down did not appeal, he was only twenty-eight, and there was plenty of time.

By the time he was reaching his third call of the day, in the early afternoon, he had worked out a plan: he would continue to soften up Josie, as he thought of it. Hopefully he would have another chance this evening as he knew she was coming to watch the performance. Saturday would have to be the night of his seduction and he would pretend his car had broken down and get her to drive him home after the last night party. He had noticed a spare tunic lying in the dressing room; he would take it home tonight and would ask her to return it for him. That would give him the excuse of inviting her into his flat, if she was as reluctant as he expected she might be. She wouldn't refuse to collect the costume as she was obviously conscientious. Job done, he reckoned. He drove home through the winding lanes

31

oblivious of the scenery and with scant regard for other road users. The thought of getting her into bed with him was worth lingering over, to the exclusion of all else. He was pleased with his plan.

Chapter 7

JOSIE'S DAY AT WORK hadn't been entirely smooth, either. All the computers in her office were suffering from some sort of problem and engineers had been called in. It wasn't until after lunch that she could get on with her normal work and then her boss had been called out on a site visit to deal with a contested planning application and she had been unable to finalise a conference he had asked her to organise as she didn't have his availability. It had all been very tedious. It didn't help that she found herself uneasy and on edge over Mike. She was half-excited and intrigued by his attentions but also aware that she hated the physical contact with him and lacked the confidence she needed to deal with him. She knew she was being pathetic but didn't know what to do. She was also going to be late home.

She walked up to her front door still pondering about Mike. There was a pink rose flowering by the step and normally she would have stopped to smell it and admire the velvety softness of the petals. It had been one of her Dad's favourites, a hybrid tea that he meticulously pruned each year at the end of February.

'You can't beat HT roses, Josie,' he would say. 'They never let you down if you prune them and feed them and treat them right.'

Tonight there was a solitary petal spinning round in the slight breeze, a little pink sail caught in a gossamer-thin strand of a spider's web. Adrift from its parent plant it was waiting for the web to snap and launch it into the air to shrivel, turn brown and rot on the edge of the lawn. But Josie was too preoccupied to notice.

She had received a text from Di during her lunch break. It asked her to go backstage before the performance and help with some last-minute costume alterations that the producer had decreed were essential. Di's tone of voice when Josie rang her back was acerbic.

'He's just making work for the sake of it, in my opinion, Josie,' she had said 'Those sashes were perfectly all right; just because that idiot in the chorus didn't fasten his properly last night and it fell off we now have to replace the pips and pops with Velcro on all of them. I'm sorry it means you have to come in early but I can't get them done on my own in the time.'

Josie had said it was fine and she would be there as near six as she could manage. Now, as she scrabbled in the bottom of her handbag for her door key, she realised that she had a bare half hour to get something to eat, to change out of her work clothes and get to the village hall. Not to mention having time to decide what to do about Mike if she were to bump in to him, which seemed rather more likely now she was going to be backstage before the performance.

Di and Josie sewed the Velcro to the sashes and finished with minutes to spare before curtain up. The men's chorus had been queuing in the passage outside the wardrobe room to collect their sashes and the atmosphere had become a little tense as the clock ticked on. Josie had been relieved when Mike arrived that he had been too preoccupied with his costume to chat her up and after a cursory glance and a 'see you after the show' thrown at her, he left the room fastening his sash. She didn't answer and he was quickly gone.

The ushers on the door directed her to a seat near the back of the hall. They weren't expecting another full house but as her seat was complimentary they wanted to keep better ones for any latecomers who were prepared to pay. Josie didn't mind, she preferred to be out of the public gaze and was hoping she didn't know anyone else in the audience as she found social chit chat rather difficult. She could never think of anything to say after initial greetings were over. She so envied other girls who seemed to be able to talk about anything or nothing for hours on end without any difficulty. Why can't I be like them? she wondered.

Seeing the show all the way through without a break, apart from the interval, was quite an eye-opener. Josie enjoyed it far more than she expected and left the hall humming away with the rest of the audience and feeling upbeat with the success. It really was quite good, she thought, though she knew she had nothing to compare it with. It had been difficult to distinguish one member of the chorus from another with their identical wigs and costumes, but she had picked Mike out and was surprised that he seemed to blend in so well and the singing was lovely, she had to admit. She almost wished she had agreed to take part after all. As she left the hall she wondered if Mike would try to waylay her but she reckoned if she was quick he wouldn't have time to remove his costume before she had gone. And so it proved.

Mike, however, was annoyed that Josie didn't turn up in the green room after the show. There was no sign of her as he started on his first lager.

'Playing hard to get, I suppose,' he thought as he drove home later. 'I'll make sure I see her before Saturday and soften her up.' His confidence was undiminished. Girls usually regretted messing him around. He didn't consider himself predatory; he hadn't really thought about it. He was only doing what blokes had always done, and always would do, wasn't he?

Saturday started as a glorious summer's day and Josie followed her normal routine. She breakfasted a bit later than usual and then set to on her chores, as she called them. They involved a quick hoover round the house, a wipe down of the kitchen surfaces whilst feeding the washing machine with her work clothes and sheets one week and towels the next. She sorted the rubbish, fed and watered the houseplants and cleaned the brass. Towards the end of the morning she drove to a nearby supermarket and bought what she needed for the next week. Later she would do the ironing and might do a bit in the garden. The roses needed deadheading, their first flush fading now. It was all very predictable and organised, but she liked that.

She was pleased with herself for managing to avoid Mike, more or less, since Tuesday evening. She was on duty in the wardrobe room during Wednesday's and Friday's performances and he had come looking for her on Wednesday, but she had been busy with another member of the chorus, sewing up an errant hem. Mike hovered around for a few moments but Josie was concentrating and he eventually left. If he had returned on Friday she was unaware – or she had been somewhere else – and he had missed her. They did pass in the passage once but he was rushing for his entrance so there was no time to chat. Josie thought maybe he had lost interest and although for a moment she felt a pang of disappointment it was transitory and she was relieved not to have to parry his advances.

By the time evening came the weather had become very humid and oppressive. All the cast were moaning about having to put on their wigs and costumes; the dressing rooms were crowded and airless and becoming more unpleasant as the evening wore on. Josie and Di were together in the wardrobe room with the door open so that they could hear the music and keep the air flowing through. Everyone was very excited, despite the heat, and it was infectious. When they heard Pitti-Sing begin the last number, 'For he's Gone and Married Yum-Yum' they squeezed their way through members of the cast waiting for the curtain calls and found a space in the wings where they could see what was going on. The audience greeted the final curtain with yells and shouts of delight; bouquets were brought on stage and presented, speeches were given and applauded and the whole atmosphere was totally over the top. Finally the audience decided to go home, whereupon Di and Josie retired back to the wardrobe room to await the avalanche of costumes that they had to sort and pack up for return to the costume hirers. It was a long, hard hour's work, not helped by the over-excited cast failing to produce all their accessories as requested. Eventually, however, they had more or less accounted for everything and had finished packing the wicker hampers.

'I think that'll do for tonight, Josie,' Di said, brushing her hair out of her eyes with a weary hand, her brow furrowed and glistening with sweat. 'Have you ticked the second sheet off?'

'All the girl's stuff's in here, but I think there's a man's tunic missing. I've counted twice.' She also sounded weary. 'Do you think it's that spare one we gave Gavin when he split the seam of his own at the dress rehearsal, do you remember?

'Could well be. Let's leave it for now, then, and do another check in the morning when the dressing rooms are empty.' Di closed the lid of the hamper resignedly.

'Okay.' Josie was happy to acquiesce.

'I could do with a drink.' Di was re-doing her lipstick and peering into the mirror on the wall. 'Are you coming? We don't want to miss all the jollities. I bet there's no food left by now anyway.'

'Just for a quick drink, maybe.' Josie was too tired to be very enthusiastic. 'What time are you coming back tomorrow?'

'Let's say 10 o'clock, shall we? It shouldn't take long.'

'That's fine.' Josie picked up her handbag and they both left the wardrobe room and hurried towards the hall where they could hear a great buzz of noise.

The green room wasn't big enough for a party with the full cast as well as their family and friends, so the producer had arranged to use the hall as soon as the audience had left and the doormen had had time to stack the chairs and set out tables along the walls. Caterers had arrived and food had been laid out. By the time Josie and Di reached the hall there wasn't much food left, as Di had predicted. She soon spotted her husband across the room so Josie was left alone looking hopefully for something to eat. She was moving along the table towards some crisps and a plate of rather tired-looking sandwiches when she was blocked by a large figure. It was Mike. He had two glasses precariously held in one hand and a plate piled high with food in the other.

'Where've you been? I've been looking for you.'

It was a peremptory question and Josie was flustered and defensive. They hadn't arranged to meet, had they?

38

'Oh. Sorry. We were sorting and packing the costumes. It took a long time, some things were missing.' She put her hand out to reach the bowl of crisps but Mike thrust a glass of wine at her and manoeuvred her away from the table into a corner near the stage.

'Here you are,' he said bossily. 'I've got lots of food. D'you want a sandwich?'

She found herself backed against the wall and with little option but to take the proffered ham sandwich and the drink. She felt increasingly uncomfortable; he was too close to her and she was trapped.

He munched his own sandwich for a moment before saying 'I'm so sorry,' he was unconvincingly apologetic, 'I think I might be to blame if you're missing a costume.' He never expected it to be this easy.

Josie looked puzzled but didn't say anything.

'Completely by mistake the other night I took one of the tunics home with me. It was muddled up with some other stuff and I didn't notice. Then I forgot to bring it back. I didn't know whose it was. I am so sorry,' he lied, looking at her and clearly expecting her to say it didn't matter.

'We have to send everything back on Monday,' she stated flatly.

'I know, I know.' He seemed to contemplate the options. 'Trouble is I haven't got my car this weekend; it's in the garage having the clutch fixed.' He looked suitably worried. 'I wonder... No, I couldn't possibly ask...' He hesitated, then seemed to make his mind up reluctantly. 'You couldn't possibly drive me home tonight, could you? Then I could give you the tunic, otherwise I can't do anything about it till Monday, and I wouldn't want to get you into trouble with the hire firm.' He leaned further over her and put on an expression of deepest concern. 'You'd be a real sweetie if you could do that for poor little me.' He put his now empty plate down on the table.

Josie tried vainly to think of an excuse to avoid driving him home but her hesitation was more than enough for Mike.

'Bless you; bless you, that's marvellous.' He patted her arm proprietorially. 'We'll go in a minute, shall we?'

'I don't know where you live,' she said helplessly.

'It's not far, on the Springfield estate, just over the bypass, takes about ten minutes.' He drained his glass.

The Springfield estate was a relatively new build, a mix of houses and flats on previously agricultural land, bordering the nearby market town where Josie worked. It more or less joined up the village of Northwood with the town, to the disgust of the Northwood residents who felt their village identity was under threat from the development. The bypass separated the two and there was another main road criss-crossing the estate. Josie drove daily along the main road on her way to work but hadn't ever been through the estate. It was considered a bit of a rabbit warren.

She started to say that she wasn't sure she could take him home when there was a loud clap of thunder clearly audible above the noisy chat in the village hall. After the hot and sultry day, following a week of mostly sunny weather, the thunderstorm was no surprise. Josie hated thunderstorms; she was frightened of the noise and she suffered from headaches that she associated with the high pressure. She wanted to be at home.

She hurriedly put her glass and empty plate down on the edge of the stage and looked up at Mike in alarm.

40

'I think I had better be getting home,' she said, and bent to pick up her handbag from the floor where she had put it.

'Good idea,' he responded. 'I'll see you to your car, come on.'

She was surprised at his seeming gallantry but was too preoccupied with the storm to think logically about it. They hurried out of the main doors and into the car park. It was quite dark by now and rain had started. Josie's little red Peugeot was parked in the far corner and as they dashed across the tarmac there was another huge thunderclap accompanied by a torrential downpour. In her haste Josie fumbled as she got her keys out of her bag and dropped them.

'Oh, no,' she wailed. 'I can't see them.'

Mike was quick to spot the metal glinting on the wet tarmac. He picked the keys up.

'Which is your car?'

'The red one, over there.' She pointed.

He sped ahead of her and used the remote to open the doors, then bundled her into the passenger seat before rushing round to the driver's door and getting in.

'You can't drive my car,' she protested as he made to slam the door shut.

He ignored her, put the keys into the ignition and turned the engine on.

'You won't be insured.' Josie's voice rose.

'You're in no fit state to drive. I'll take you home and get a taxi back.' He switched the car lights on.

'No, no.' She absolutely did not want Mike to know where she lived 'What about the tunic?'

He was pulling out of the car park and into the road. He braked suddenly to let another car pass.

'Oh damn the bloody tunic.' He whistled through his teeth in pretended exasperation. 'Okay, I'll drive to my flat, get it and then drive you home. It won't take long.'

Josie winced involuntarily at the expletive but more than anything she wanted to get Mike out of her car.

'There's no need to take me home. Maybe the thunder will have stopped.' She was hopeful. She clutched her handbag tightly. 'Honestly, I'll be fine.'

'Okay, okay,' he said again and changed into third gear then slammed the windscreen wipers onto their fastest setting.

The car's seat belt alarm went off.

'You haven't got your seat belt on.' Josie was increasingly anxious and her voice rose again.

With an infuriated sigh Mike buckled up. He ignored Josie's anxiety as he mentally planned how to inveigle her into his flat when they got there. He was also trying to remember where he had put the tunic; it would obviously have to be produced.

The drive didn't take long but the rain didn't ease up and it was bucketing down when Mike turned into the driveway of the flats. He circled round so that the car was parked facing the road. He put on the handbrake and switched everything off.

Josie expected him to leave her in the car while he fetched the tunic and, as he got out, she started to switch seats ready to drive off again, but he was round to her side and opening the passenger door before she could do so. He yanked at her arm.

'Come on, get out,' he insisted. 'You can't sit in here in a thunderstorm, come inside and wait for it to ease.' He pulled her out and more or less manhandled her to the communal door.

She had no choice, and moments later they were in the hallway of his flat. He pushed open a door ahead of them and switched on a light in what turned out to be the kitchen.

He crossed the room and drew the blind, blotting out the intermittent lightning flashes. Josie glanced around the kitchen. It was an awful mess, she thought. Obviously Mike didn't spend Saturday mornings on housework as she did. There were plates and dishes piled in the sink; takeaway cartons heaped on the work surface by the dirty cooker and various cans of lager stacked on the floor. She shuddered at the squalor. 'Please let him find the tunic quickly and then I can go home.' Her feelings of disquiet increased when she remembered he still had her car keys.

Mike was looking in the fridge and brought out a half-finished bottle of chardonnay. He searched in a cupboard for clean glasses, failed to find any and picked up two rather tea-stained mugs from the draining board. He poured out large measures of wine and handed one mug to Josie. He took a big slurp from the other.

'Come and sit down in here.' He opened a door off the kitchen and led the way into an equally untidy sitting room. He pushed a load of papers off a black leather sofa onto the floor, making enough space for Josie to sit.

'I'll just find the tunic.' He put his mug down and left the room; Josie assumed he had gone to his bedroom.

She glanced nervously around before hesitantly perching on the edge of the sofa, her untouched drink in her hand. As he didn't return immediately she jumped up again and darted back into the kitchen; it was with enormous relief that she saw her car keys on the work surface by the fridge. Mike must have put them down when he opened the bottle. Hastily, and glancing over her shoulder as she did so, she stuffed them into her trouser pocket at the same time tipping her wine into the sink. She moved towards the door to the hall but as she did so Mike returned with the tunic in one hand and his half-empty mug in the other.

'You're not going.' It was a statement rather than a question. 'Look. I found it. I knew I had put it somewhere safe.' He came towards her.

She held out her hand to take the tunic but he waved it away from her, out of reach.

'Hey, no, you're not going,' he repeated putting his drink down by the sink and quickly stepped between her and the door.

'Yes, I must.' Josie tried to leave but he grabbed her with his free hand and pulled her roughly to him.

'You're much too pretty to be leaving just yet,' he murmured, his mouth close to her ear. 'C'mon, Josie, we've got lots in common, you and me. Let's have a bit of fun.' He dropped the tunic on the floor and cupped her left breast with his now free hand.

'No, no,' Josie screamed. She struggled frantically in protest.

'Oh, yes,' he massaged her breast and at the same time pulled her closer to him with his other hand on her buttocks. He ground himself against her.

His mouth found hers and his tongue forced her lips apart. The taste of wine from his mouth and the aroma of unwashed male body repulsed her. She tried to pull herself away but he was too strong and the kiss seemed unending. He pushed his tongue down her throat.

Eventually he stopped for air and Josie tried again to break free.

'Let me go, let me go.' She battered her hands impotently against his chest.

'Not just yet.' He was grinning down at her. He moved his hand from her breast and groped at the front opening of her trousers and with remarkable dexterity unzipped them and pushed his hand between her legs.

She was terrified and tried to wriggle from his intrusive fingers but he backed her against the wall and pinned her with his body as he kissed her again. Panic rose within her. She had to get away; she couldn't bear his hands on her. Instinctively, using all her strength, she freed her own hands and pushed them hard into Mike's face; he backed fractionally away and as he did so she lifted her left knee and rammed it as hard as she could into his groin. He yelled and staggered further back.

'You frigid little bitch,' he screamed bending double in pain, releasing her.

She turned and fled through the hall and out into the pouring rain. Somehow she got the keys out of her pocket with one hand and, clutching her unzipped trousers with the other, she hurled herself at the car door, unlocked it and stumbled in just as Mike appeared at the front door yelling at her, his face red and furious. The car's engine roared into life, she floored the accelerator and steered out into the road turning violently left. For a moment she couldn't remember which way they had come. All she wanted was to get out of his sight and away from his flat. She was hyperventilating but oblivious of her surroundings, aware only of her terrible, urgent, need to escape. The rain was slashing at the window, obliterating everything.

Something happened.

Josie felt a bump on the nearside front wing of the car. She swerved automatically. She had no idea what it was and in her overwhelming panic she could think of nothing but getting away from Mike and back to the safety of her own home. It didn't occur to her to stop. Shortly after, she realised she hadn't switched on the car lights or wipers and was appalled at her own negligence. She slowed down and drove more carefully, checking every so often in case there was a car following her. The relief when she reached her house was enormous. Quickly she parked and got out of the car. The thunderstorm was passing, the rain had eased to a steady drizzle. She looked warily round as she hurried up the path, half expecting Mike to appear. Then she remembered he had said his car was in the garage being mended. Maybe that was a lie? Maybe he would follow her? She wished she didn't have to leave her car in front of the house where he could see it. Hastily she unlocked her front door and even more hastily shut and locked it again behind her. She leaned against the locked door and drew breath; she was still shaking and now felt very cold. Perhaps a hot bath would help?

Somehow she managed to get upstairs and into the bathroom; she turned the taps on. She took off all her clothes and put them in the laundry basket. No way could she wear any of them tomorrow; they felt contaminated.

She sploshed a liberal amount of bath essence into the hot water and it foamed up comfortingly. She stepped into the bath and lay down. Why had it happened? What had she done to encourage Mike to behave like that? Had she led him on in some way? She went back over the evening, trying to remember everything they had said to each other. There didn't seem to be anything to trigger his attack. It was completely inexplicable but she reached the conclusion that somehow it must have been her fault. She must have led him on, albeit unwittingly. Now what should she do? She felt so deeply ashamed of herself. No one must know what a fool she was. She needn't see Mike again if she left the operatic society, and he didn't know where she lived. The whole business must be blotted out. It was too painful.

'What an utter fool I am.' She spoke out loud as she vigorously washed herself with her flannel, trying unconsciously to wipe away any physical evidence of him.

Fifteen minutes later she was just getting into bed, feeling a bit better, when the front door bell rang. Josie froze, and looked at her bedside clock. A quarter past midnight. Surely it couldn't be Mike? She felt her fear return. What if it was him? Perhaps she had better not answer the door. But whoever it was would have seen her bedroom light and would know she was at home. What should she do? She was shivering, undecided, when the bell rang again, more urgently this time. Then she heard the letter box flap opening. A man's voice called through.

'Open the door, please. Police.'

Police? Why? Had Mike called them? Why would he do that? Had she hurt him badly and he was in hospital? She felt scared. She wrapped herself in her dressing gown and went downstairs. Her head was spinning, trying in vain to think of reasons for such a late-night visit from the police. She put on the hall light and could see a face through the centre pane of the door; it wasn't Mike's face. She unlocked the door cautiously.

'Josephine Anderson?' A youngish man in a dark suit stood on the step holding identification out to her. Behind him were two uniformed police constables, a young man and an even younger woman. She would remember the raindrops glinting on their uniforms illuminated by the hall light.

'Yes.'

'I'm Detective Constable Andrew Morris and these are my colleagues. May we come in?'

Not waiting for a reply they all came into Josie's hallway and the woman officer shut the door.

'Josephine Anderson, I am arresting you on suspicion of causing death by dangerous driving. You do not have to say anything but it may harm your defence if you do not mention when questioned something you later rely on in court...'

Chapter 8

BEING SUCKED INTO the criminal justice system was a terrifying process, Josie found on the night she was arrested. She had been permitted to get dressed before being driven to the police station in the back of the marked police car. On the way there, only a fifteen-minute drive, her mind was still racing. The officers didn't speak to her and she didn't have the courage to ask them what was supposed to have happened. How could she have killed anyone? It didn't sound as if Mike was involved, which was a relief. She remembered the bump on the side of the car, but surely she hadn't hit anyone? She would have known, wouldn't she? She would have seen them? Her agonising was stopped short by their arrival at the police station. She was bundled out of the car and into the custody suite where her details were taken. Inevitably she was fingerprinted, breathalysed and tested for drugs. The readings were negative.

For the next couple of hours she sat in a gloomy little interview room facing D. C. Morris and his female colleague. She was asked if she wanted a solicitor but she said she didn't.

Josie was told that a witness had seen a car, probably red, certainly a Peugeot, driving without lights on near a pedestrian crossing controlled by traffic lights in the Springfield estate; he had noted part of the number plate. Another witness claimed to have seen a youngish man waiting to cross the road at the lights. The same man was found in the road moments later with severe injuries consistent with being hit by a car. As he fell he had hit his head on the edge of the kerb. He had died almost immediately after reaching hospital.

Hearing this information Josie had gone white with shock. D. C. Andrew Morris had persisted with his questioning and she agreed she had a red Peugeot. She agreed she had been driving in the area. She couldn't remember the traffic lights. She told him that she was driving home. She volunteered the information that she had felt a bump. She agreed that she hadn't stopped. She said she had been completely unaware of hitting anyone.

D.C. Morris had looked at his colleague incredulously. Here was a suspect actually volunteering incriminating evidence. He told her that her car would be examined by forensics.

Josie could think of nothing except 'I...have...killed...a ...man'. This stark fact rolled round and round in her head obliterating everything else. It never occurred to her to deny anything or prevaricate. 'If they are saying I hit and killed someone then I must have done so.'

She was taken to a cell and given a cup of tea. The cell was bare, the only furniture was a built-in platform where she could sit or lie down. There was a grey blanket folded on the platform. The thunderstorm had cleared the air but it was still a warm night. It was noisy; she could hear shouting and swearing coming from other cells and feet tramping up and down outside her door endlessly. Despite the warmth of the night she wrapped herself in the grey, scratchy blanket and lay down. She couldn't think; she couldn't cry; she couldn't do anything except wait like a condemned man.

Some hours later, grey with exhaustion, she was taken back to the interviewing room and the questioning began again.

'Where had you been last night?'

'Where were you going?

'Why weren't your lights on?'

'Who had you been to see?'

'What happened?'

On and on it went. Josie told them about the last night party. She told them she went to fetch a missing costume. She wouldn't give them Mike's name or address. Not to protect him but because she couldn't bear to remember her own stupidity and she didn't want any further involvement with him.

Again and again they asked her where she had been and with whom.

'I must keep him out of it,' was her overwhelming thought. 'I cannot explain the events in his flat; I have to block it out. I cannot talk about it. I cannot tell anyone how stupid and naive I was. I don't ever want to see him again. I couldn't face him in a court room and be cross-examined about what happened.' The memory of his hands on her body was too raw.

Finally they let her go. Someone drove her home. She was bailed 'pending further enquiries' and her car was taken away. She was advised to contact a solicitor.

Chapter 9

IT WAS EARLY NOVEMBER and Josie was standing in the Crown Court dock. The rail surrounding the dock was wooden; the wood was dark from the sweat stains of many hands clutching it over many years. Men and women, some convicted of appalling crimes and sentenced appropriately, others found innocent after long and gruelling trials, had stood where Josie was now standing. Their knees would have trembled, their pulses raced and perspiration would have poured from their brows as they waited for the judge to pronounce sentence.

Nothing was different for Josie. She appeared calm and controlled but it was a façade. She was wearing a dark suit and a white blouse, her hair was tied back in a neat ponytail making her look younger than her thirty-two years. Her hands, though, clutching the dock rail, were white at the knuckles and the support given by the rail was essential in stopping her knees from buckling under her. Her breathing, audible only to the security guard standing alongside her, was rapid and shallow. There were sweat beads on her hairline. Somehow she managed to look straight at the judge, unblinking.

The judge, wearing black and purple with a wide scarlet sash from shoulder to waist, was sitting opposite her on a raised dais. A low shaft of wintry sunshine shone through the high, narrow windows beside him; motes of dust shimmied in the air and the sunlight flickered on his grey wig. He adjusted his spectacles then looked straight back at her.

'Josephine Anderson, you pleaded guilty to causing death by careless driving.' He paused for a moment and looked at his notes. Resuming, he said 'I have thought long and hard about your case. You have provided no mitigation for your actions on the evening of 25 July. Yet you have spared witnesses from giving evidence in a distressing case by pleading guilty and for that I commend you. In pleading guilty you have also spared the state from a possibly long and certainly costly trial. You are also of previous good character.'

He paused again and took a drink of water from the tumbler by his right hand. Josie waited, seemingly impassive.

'You admitted to drinking one glass of wine on that evening. You were, however, driving without lights on. It was a dark, wet night at around 11.30. There was a considerable amount of other road traffic that Saturday night. You stated that you did not have your windscreen wipers on despite the heavy rain. Your speed was not excessive but you failed to stop at a red light at a pedestrian crossing. Then you failed to stop after an accident having told the court that you were aware of a bump to the nearside of your vehicle. You failed to report the accident.

'I am extremely puzzled at your failure to provide an explanation of your actions that evening. Your pre-sentence report from the Probation Service does not assist me greatly in reaching a decision. Tragically, however, it is the case that you killed an innocent man as he attempted quite legitimately to cross the road. The charge, as you know, was commuted from one of causing death by dangerous driving to that of causing death by careless driving. Nonetheless, considering all the factors in this case, and despite your obvious remorse, I have no alternative but to sentence you to an immediate custodial sentence.'

He paused yet again, then said: 'You are sentenced to a period of custody at Her Majesty's pleasure of twelve months, of which you will serve half.'

There was a gasp from the few people in the public gallery.

The judge raised his head and looked at them. 'You will understand that this penalty in no way reflects the deep suffering that Mr Brodinski's family must be experiencing.'

There were more details about how the sentence would operate and about a driving disqualification, but Josie wasn't listening. She had retreated into herself in shock.

From far away she heard the judge say 'Take her down,' and then she became aware of the guard putting handcuffs on her wrists and negotiating her out of the dock and down the grimy staircase to the cells.

Chapter 10

THE TANNOY BLARED OUT.

'Would the following ladies report immediately to the Education Department for the commencement of their induction.'

Josie and Joyce left the relative warmth and familiarity of their adjacent rooms and apprehensively made their way together across the campus. Their first daytime view of Edgehill Prison was depressing but they were too preoccupied to notice much about their surroundings; getting to the right place at the right time without attracting attention was priority.

The prison was laid out over thirty acres of land. There was a muddle of Nissan-type huts, concrete office blocks and some low, one-storey brick-built buildings, seemingly dotted hap-hazardously anywhere where development had been decreed by successive administrations. In November it was a bleak, cold, unwelcoming environment.

The air hung thick with fog, shrouding the scurrying prisoners as they made their way to work. Trees, lining the paths to the education block, stood skeletal in the mist, overhanging flower beds where uncut brown stems of exhausted perennials and long-dead bedding plants drooped drearily. The weedy undergrowth was home only to the resident sparrow population that flitted hopefully from stem to bough in the hope of an unsuspecting insect. Grey-brown birds sentenced to life in a grey-brown landscape. Except the birds were not sentenced; they were free to fly perkily over the twenty-foot steel perimeter fences that encircled the campus; they were undeterred by the razor wire fixed on top of the fences impeding those inside from escaping and those outside from, sometimes successfully, propelling illicit substances into the prison. Nor were the birds imprisoned by an inner fence that was sporadically punctuated by big metal gates, locked at night but opened daily to allow free movement for the women as they lived out their sentences. The sparrows cheeped cheerily, possibly in defiance of HMPS regulations.

The Education Block, where Josie and Joyce were heading, had a gravel path leading to double doors that were plastered with posters advertising a variety of courses on offer, most of them out of date. Other women were making their way inside and Josie and Joyce followed and found themselves in a classroom with about a dozen tables ranged around the walls and a harassed-looking woman waiting with a clipboard in her hand beside an old-fashioned blackboard. They were told to sign in on the clipboard and then sit down.

For the next three hours, punctuated by a brief stop for coffee, the dozen women were subjected to a barrage of information, most of which they failed to assimilate. They were all new inmates, first-time prisoners, and were in varying degrees of shock or trauma at finding themselves incarcerated. Some were crying, some were argumentative, some defiant. Josie, more miserable than she had ever imagined it was possible to be, remained silent, trying to be invisible, trying to avoid offering any information about herself to anyone. She had never, ever, felt so wretched.

'All right, everyone, that's enough for this morning. We'll

resume after lunch, back here please at 1.15.' The harassed-looking woman put down her folder and ushered the twelve prisoners out of the door, which she then locked with the key from the chain round her waist.

Josie was one of the last to leave.

'Where do we go for lunch?' she asked timidly.

'Go back to your house and wait for the tannoy to call you, then follow the others,' was the curt reply.

Joyce, who had been listening to this exchange, her eyes wide with apprehension, grabbed Josie's arm.

'Can I come with you?' she pleaded.

Josie nodded and together they made their way back to Beech House. They sat on Josie's bed and waited until an announcement came telling them to go to the dining room. They hurried across the campus and found a large brick-built building with doors at both ends and big windows running along the whole of one side. There were tables four deep across the room with red chairs in regimented order, eight to a table, neatly pushed in except where they were already occupied by women who were busy having lunch. Behind a counter at the far end were heated cabinets of food and white-clad prisoners distributing it to a lengthy queue. The kitchen was behind. Four prison officers were leaning against the side wall chatting amongst themselves, but clearly keeping a close eye on what was going on.

It was warm in the dining room and the windows were steamy from hot food and breath. Josie found herself relaxing slightly and, as she smelled the food, she realised that she was very hungry. Gradually they reached the head of the queue and could see what was on offer. It didn't look too bad. Joyce chose a plate of pasta bake and Josie asked for savoury mince. They moved to a side table to collect a drink of water but as Josie turned to see where to sit she collided with another woman and her plate went spinning onto the floor and the mince splattered everywhere. She felt the other woman's leg twine round her own and the next moment she fell headlong onto the wooden floor in an ignominious heap. She knew it had been a deliberate collision but realised that to the prison officers it would seem she had just been clumsy. She tried to scramble to her feet but her assailant blocked her.

'Oh, bad luck, you fuckin' posh bitch,' the woman mocked her, pushing her to the floor again; other prisoners crowded round egging on the perpetrator and masking her so that the watching officers were unable to see who was responsible for the melee. Joyce tried, ineffectually, to pull the woman away from Josie but in her turn was shoved aside by two more prisoners.

'Get up, you,' an officer strode over and shouted at Josie. 'Get a mop and clean this mess up. Behave yourself or I'll put you on report. Get back to your lunch, the rest of you.'

'It wasn't 'er fault,' Joyce screamed, her face puce with fury. 'That woman tripped 'er up.' She jabbed her finger at the assailant who was smirking. The smirk turned to anger and the woman launched herself at Joyce. Two more officers intervened and Joyce and the woman were pulled apart, both shouting in protest.

Josie got slowly to her feet. Grey blobs of congealing mince clung greasily to her trousers and her hands stank; she tried to clean them with her handkerchief. The dining room had quietened and all the prisoners were watching intently to see what would happen next. Josie wanted the ground to open up and swallow her. Someone shoved a wet mop into her hand; someone else retrieved the unbroken plate. The officers released Joyce and the other woman with warnings to both. Somehow Josie cleaned up the mince and then found herself sitting at a table with Joyce and with a new plate of food in front of her. She was too scared to lift her eyes from her plate and concentrated on eating as fast as she could. Her assailant seemed to have disappeared.

Sitting on her bed fifteen minutes later with Joyce beside her, Josie was shaken. That had been awful. Why did that woman call her a 'posh bitch'? She wanted to curl up on her bed and never, ever, meet that prisoner again, or the others who had jeered at her. She gazed at the cracked linoleum on the floor. Then she remembered Joyce.

'Thanks for helping and standing up for me,' she said diffidently, still looking at the floor.

'S'all right, we need to stick together for now, don' we?' Her Welsh lilt was more pronounced.

'Why did she do it, do you think?'

'Just 'cos we're new, I s'pose.'

'Maybe.'

There was silence for a while.

Josie made an effort to concentrate on something else; she turned to Joyce.

'I've been meaning to ask you...' She paused.

'What?'

'Was it you crying in the van on the way here?'

Joyce looked sideways at her through a curtain of hair.

'Mm.' It was her turn to look at the floor.

'What had upset you so much? I mean weren't you

expecting to go to prison?'

'Oh, yeah. I dunno. Like it just seemed so final, yer know; banged up in the cells then pushed on the van, locked in that little box; couldn't move, couldn't breathe; I didn't even get to say goodbye to me Mam. Lots of stuff.' She spread her hands across her knees and her shoulders sank dejectedly. 'Also,' she spoke more quietly, 'I needed me meds.'

'What did you do? To be in here, I mean?' Josie asked, puzzled, then, wondering if she had gone too far 'Don't tell me if you'd rather not.'

'S'all right. Drug dealing.'

'Oh.'

'So, what are you in for?'

'I killed a man in a road accident.'

'Blimey. How long d'yer get, then?'

'Twelve months. You?'

'Eighteen.'

They sat in silence again, both sunk in their own thoughts until Josie looked at her watch.

'We'd better be going back.' She got up reluctantly and Joyce followed her to the door.

'We'll stick together,' Joyce said. It was a statement.

That night Josie went to bed physically tired out but her mind was still racing, trying to make sense of her new life. Should she have implicated Mike in her court case by explaining what had happened in his flat? Would that have been mitigation for driving so badly and hitting the man? Would the judge have been lenient? Would she have had some sort of community punishment, which was what her barrister had led her to believe she would receive? She dejectedly pulled her duvet further up round her shoulders.

'Oh, Josie, Josie, what a fool you are,' she sobbed out loud. 'What would Dad say to me now if he could see me?' She turned restlessly onto her back. 'He'd tell me to pull myself together and try and make the best of a bad job. But how can I? I don't think I can last six days in here, let alone six months.'

Sleep continued to elude her as she listened to the unfamiliar noises in the passage outside her locked door. She could hear footsteps clumping along the concrete path beneath her window, now screened, somewhat inadequately, by the scruffy bit of curtain Michelle had given her. There was the gruff voice of a prison officer, who must have had a guard dog with him, saying: 'This way, Rex, good boy,' followed by the inevitable clanging of keys on a chain.

She turned onto her other side, trying to find a comfortable position in the narrow bed. She remembered the day after the accident.

The police officers had dropped her off at her front door when they had finished interviewing her. It had been mid-morning on the Sunday and Josie had been terrified that her neighbours would have seen a police car pull up. She had rushed indoors and then not known what to do. She was hungry and exhausted but she couldn't focus on anything except that she had killed a man and would have to face the consequences. She paced round the kitchen, then she went into the sitting room, then she went upstairs, then down again. Over and over she muttered the words, first soundlessly, then as she became increasingly agitated she found she was shouting 'I have killed a man'. Finally, she slumped into her chair at the kitchen table and sobbed until she was completely drained. She put her arms on the table and laid her head on them and shut her eyes. Perhaps it was just a nightmare after all and she would wake up in her normal world again tomorrow. Then she heard a buzz from her mobile phone. It was in her bag on a chair just inside the kitchen door. Wearily she got up and fetched it; there were three missed calls, all from Di.

'Oh my God,' she spoke aloud. 'I should have been at the village hall this morning. What can I tell Di? No, I can't tell her.'

Perhaps she could say she was ill? But what about the tunic? As she was trying to think of plausible excuses the phone in the hall rang. Josie hurried over to it and then paused, her hand almost on the receiver as she tried to think of the implications of not answering the call. Finally, just before the answer phone clicked in she lifted the receiver.

'Hello?' she said faintly.

'Josie, it's Di, I've been trying your mobile all morning and you didn't pick up. Are you all right?' Di sounded part worried and part annoyed.

There was a long pause before Josie replied, 'Yes, I'm all right.'

'Well, where have you been? There was so much to do this morning and you said you'd be there at ten.'

'I know, I'm sorry, something happened.' Josie's voice was flat.

'What happened? What do you mean? You don't sound right. What is it?'

There was no reply.

'What's the matter?'

There was still no reply.

Di said 'Shall I come round?'

'No, yes, Oh, I don't know.'

'I'm coming. Be with you in ten minutes.' The phone went dead.

Josie looked at the receiver in her hand.

'I can't tell her the truth, not about Mike, it's too awful, but what can I say? She'll see me like this and know it's something dreadful. They'll all know sooner or later, but not about Mike, I can't say anything about him. They'll think I'm such a fool...'

Di parked her car in the road and walked quickly up to the front door. She had dropped Josie off after rehearsals a couple of times but had never been inside her house. She noted the neat front garden, a trimmed privet hedge bordering the road, a line of begonias flanking the path like little pink sentries standing neatly to attention and a couple of hybrid tea roses each side of the door, both coming to the end of their first flowering. She rang the bell.

Her first thought on seeing Josie was that someone in her family must have died. Josie looked awful; her face was blotchy, her eyes red rimmed and her hair lank. Di tried to remember what Josie had told her about her relations but could only think of her parents, and she knew they had both died.

They went into the kitchen. Di pushed Josie gently into a chair by the table and sat opposite her.

'What's happened, Josie?'

Josie looked at her and then put her head onto the table and encircled it with her arms as if to blot everything out. She started sobbing again. Di waited a minute then got up and went round the table and put her arm round Josie's shoulder and gave her a tiny shake.

'Come on.' She crouched down beside Josie so that she could half see her face. 'I'm sure it's not that bad, but I can't help unless you tell me what it is.'

Finally, after more encouragement and a glass of water, Josie sat upright and Di drew up a chair and sat so that their knees were nearly touching. She held Josie's hand.

'It's something to do with Mike, isn't it?'

Josie looked at her in surprise. 'How did you know?'

'I saw you leaving the hall with him last night.'

Slowly, with much prompting, Josie told Di about the accident. She said nothing of Mike's assault.

Di was aghast. This was far worse than she had imagined. She sat in silence for a while still holding Josie's hand in hers and massaging it absentmindedly with her other hand. Something wasn't right. Josie was not the kind of person who behaved erratically; she was conscientious, methodical and very cautious. Timid might also be a good description. She was the last person you would expect to get into a car and drive without using lights or windscreen wipers. Di hazarded a guess.

'What was Mike doing when you left his flat?'

'I don't know.' Josie was uncomfortable.

'Did he give you the tunic?'

'No.'

'What did he do to you, Josie?'

Josie started crying again and Di could barely make out her muffled reply.

'Nothing, not really, it was my fault.'

'What did he do, Josie?' Di was more insistent.

Josie shook her head 'It was my fault.'

'What was your fault? Di looked at her intently 'Did he try and get you into bed?'

'I can't talk about it.'

'I am guessing, and you can tell me if I am right or not, that he made a pass at you, that he pushed his luck too far and you made a run for it. Am I near the truth?'

'It was my fault; I was such a fool.' Di had to bend her head to hear the whispered words.

'Predatory bastard,' she muttered more to herself than to Josie. 'What have you told the police about Mike, Josie?

'Nothing.'

'Why not?'

'I never, ever want to see him or have anything to do with him again. Not ever.' She spoke now with aggression. Then her voice trailed off and she put her head on her arms again in defeat. 'I have been so stupid.'

'But he's the reason you hit the man. You must tell the police, it makes all the difference.' Di was incredulous.

'No, no, I can't.' Josie's voice rose in panic.

Di tried to get her to see sense but Josie wouldn't shift and ultimately, after saying all she could to get her to change her mind, but with no success, Di resignedly got up to go.

'You need a good solicitor,' she said briskly and wrote a name and address on a bit of paper and thrust it into Josie's hand. 'Ring him in the morning and let me know how you get on.' Feeling frustrated and puzzled by the other woman's stubbornness she patted her on the shoulder and left.

After Di had gone Josie sat for a while at the kitchen table and began to try and work out the consequences of her arrest. The sergeant had said that they would probably be charging her with causing death by dangerous driving.

They said she would have to appear at the Magistrate's Court and then the case would be sent to the Crown Court. They said it would be three or four months, probably, before sentence. They advised her to get a solicitor.

Josie looked at the name on the piece of paper that Di had given her. David Owens, it said. Slowly Josie wrote beside the name 'ring tomorrow'. Underneath she wrote 'tell Doug'. She had realised that the local paper would very likely headline the accident in its Monday edition and she needed to tell Doug Fairview, her boss, before he read it in the paper. How to tell him? What to say? She agonised and tried out various phrases: ' I am sorry to tell you that I have been involved in an accident and shall need time off work' to 'I'm afraid something awful has happened and I am giving you my resignation...' To say, bluntly, the words 'I have killed a man' seemed too difficult. Would she be sacked with immediate effect? What would she do then? Would her name be in the local paper? How to explain that the police had taken her car?

By bedtime she had made no headway, made no telephone calls and had a raging headache. Could she run away? Where could she go? She gave no thought to the man she had killed, so wrapped up and self-absorbed was she in her own misery. She trailed dejectedly up to bed to face another sleepless night.

Lying in her prison bed four months later and reliving the awful hours after the accident gave Josie no comfort. She tossed and turned until she saw grey streaks of dawn through her dreary curtains and heard the unfamiliar noises of early morning prison life; she wearily crawled out of bed.

Chapter 11

D I HAD BEEN INFURIATED with Josie's stubbornness. 'What a stupid girl,' she had said to her husband later in the evening as he was peeling potatoes at the sink.

'She'll end up going to prison when it should be that wretched man in the dock. I knew he was a bad lot and I should have tried harder to warn Josie, she's such an innocent.' Di banged cutlery and plates on to the table ready for their evening meal.

Peter looked at his wife and shook his head. He half-filled a saucepan with water and put the potatoes into it.

'You can't nanny people, you know, it doesn't work, they have to make their own mistakes and learn by them.'

'True, but this is a mighty big mistake and the consequences are going to be horrendous.' Di put salt in the pan and placed it on the hob. She turned on the gas.

'So what are you going to do?'

'I think I'll have a word with Mike.'

'Really?' He raised an eyebrow in surprise. 'Be careful, then.' He dried his hands thoughtfully on the kitchen towel.

The following evening after she had returned from work and when she reckoned Mike should also be back Di drove to his flat.

Mike had done very little on the Sunday, the day after Josie had kicked him. His groin was still feeling pretty sore and he was annoyed at the outcome of his seduction plans. He also felt very sorry for himself. It never occurred to him that he might have had any responsibility for upsetting Josie.

She had obviously misread his signals. He got up late and lazed the day away without achieving anything.

Monday came and he set off in his car, later than intended, for North Wales, where he had four potential clients to see. By mid-afternoon he was on his way home again with two firm orders and two negative responses. He wasn't best pleased but reckoned he could justify his lack of success when he saw his manager in the morning by saying that two farmers were still thinking about his offers and he would hear from them shortly, and he was sure there would be good news by the end of the week. He knew his manager would be away on Thursday and Friday so that would give him a bit more leeway before the bad news had to be imparted. The firm wasn't doing very well and redundancy threatened if he didn't improve his sales.

He decided to stop and pick up a Chinese takeaway on his way home; there was, as usual, no food in the flat. He pulled up at the brightly lit shop on the Springfield estate and sighed when he saw there were several other customers ahead of him in the queue. He gave his order and then sat on one of the white plastic chairs lined up on the side of the room to wait for it. There was a copy of that evening's local paper folded on the table in front of him. He picked it up to check the football results on the back page but as he turned it over his eye was caught by the front-page banner headline 'Migrant killed by hit and run driver, woman held by police'. It was followed by details of the traffic lights near his flat and the time the accident had happened. Mike read on with a sense of foreboding.

Josie wasn't named but the make, model and colour of her car were; it had to be her. He was jolted from his perusal of the paper by hearing his name called; he rose from the chair and went to the counter to collect the white plastic bag with his sweet and sour chicken and noodles. His hunger had evaporated, but he took the bag and left the takeaway still clutching the evening paper.

Three minutes later he was sitting on his sofa with a can of lager in one hand and a fork in the other eating the chicken, but barely tasting it, as he re-read the article with the paper propped up in front of him.

'Bloody hell,' he spoke out loud through a mouthful of noodles. 'Stupid little bitch. How could she have been such a fucking idiot?' He took several large gulps of the lager. He began to work out the implication: would Josie have told them his name? He had no reason to suppose she wouldn't do that, it's what he would have done in her place to lay blame elsewhere. He checked his phone. Nothing new on his Facebook page as yet; that was a relief.

He started to imagine a police interview. He supposed they might well come round to see him, maybe even this evening. He had better have his story ready. Would it look better not to have heard about the accident or to have read the paper? He needed to think that through.

'No, Officer, I had no idea; what a terrible thing to happen. It's usually so quiet round here; very nice people and a nice neighbourhood. I've been out all day, I've had a very busy day and yesterday I was at home working, so heard nothing. No, I didn't see the Midlands news.'

Or: 'Yes, Officer, I do know Miss Anderson slightly. She had called round to collect a missing costume but she was only here for a minute; she was very concerned about the thunderstorm and I advised her to get home quickly. You know what girls can be like about thunderstorms (knowing man-to-man chuckle). Yes, in fact she forgot the costume and I was going to take it to the village hall in the next day or two. I think she put it down when she picked up her car keys and I didn't notice, which was silly of me. She was in such a hurry to get home. I am so sorry, how really awful (concerned frown).'

He shoved his half-eaten cartons of food away from him and drained the can of lager. As he got up to fetch another can from the fridge the doorbell rang.

'Oh God, they've come.' He hastily shoved the newspaper under the sofa cushion and went to the door. He wasn't sure whether to be relieved or not when he found Di on the doorstep.

'Can I come in?' she said before he had opened his mouth, and she pushed past him and into the sitting room.

He decided to play for time whilst finding out why she had come. 'I assume you want the tunic? It's here somewhere.' He spoke conversationally. Turning away from her he pretended to look round the room for it before spotting it on the chair where he had flung it furiously on Saturday night. He handed it to her. 'I'm so sorry I didn't bring it back yesterday, pure forgetfulness, I was so busy, work, you know.' He put on an innocent-sounding voice. 'It went well on Saturday, don't you think?'

Di took the tunic without looking at it. 'You know what's happened to Josie, don't you?' she faced him, glaring. Lying sod, she thought.

'Has something happened to Josie?' He widened his eyes innocently and looked enquiringly at her.

Di pursed her lips and spoke tartly. 'After she left you on Saturday evening she was involved in a road accident.'

70

'How awful. Is she all right?' He put on the concerned face he had been saving for the police.

'No, she's not all right and nor is some poor man she knocked over and killed. I know very well that you are responsible for this tragedy, so don't try and deny it.' Di moved a step closer to him and pushed her face right into his. 'Don't you tell me that you didn't try and seduce her on Saturday night and that caused her to panic and rush off. Then this ghastly accident happens.'

Di shoved him in the chest with her free hand.

'Get off me,' he shouted, deliberately overreacting. He thrust her away. 'How dare you come here and accuse me of something so totally ludicrous. Get out now.'

His righteous indignation was more than she could cope with. 'Oh, I'm going,' she shouted back, 'but you'd better realise that if you don't tell the police of your involvement I certainly shall.'

'I'll certainly tell the police that you're harassing me and then we'll see who gets charged.' Mike was white lipped with genuine fury. He took her arm and hauled her to the front door. 'You've no proof of any of this; it's total slander.' He pushed her out and slammed the door shut.

'Damn and bloody hell,' Di muttered as she got into her car. 'I couldn't have made a worse mess of that if I'd tried. Still, maybe I've scared the shit out of him. We'll see.' She turned on the ignition and drove out onto the road. 'At least I've got the tunic back.' She allowed herself a small wry smile and glanced at it on the seat beside her.

'Oleaginous, slimy toad,' she said to Peter as they were eating supper later. 'I can't decide what really gets me about him. I knew he was lying from the word go, but he turned the charm on as if I was only there to fetch the wretched costume when he must have known the real reason. Then to pretend he hadn't heard what had happened – that took the biscuit, I must say.' She took a drink of water. 'It's probably all over social media and I bet he checks it every five minutes, not to mention the local news and papers.'

'What are you going to do now?' Peter looked at her enquiringly.

'Not sure.' She put her glass down. 'Probably give the police a ring. Maybe have another go at getting Josie to tell them.'

'Good luck,' he said, looking sceptical.

Mike didn't like to admit it, even to himself, but he was rattled by Di's visit. He went to the fridge to get another lager but decided he needed something stronger so poured himself a very large measure of single malt. He returned to the sitting room and turned on the TV to see the local news. There was a brief mention of the accident and the fact that the police were likely to be charging a local woman with causing death by dangerous driving.

He took several large gulps of his drink and tried to think through his plan of action.

Should he contact Josie? No, he discarded that. He didn't want to see her anyway, silly bitch.

Should he pre-empt her by telling the police himself of his involvement? No, if she was going to tell them she would have done it by now, he reasoned. Best keep quiet.

If she was going to press charges for assault surely she would have done that too, by now?

Di had said she would contact the police. Would she? He thought she probably would, she was obviously very angry and what had Josie told her? If the police come round this evening or tomorrow what strategy would be best?

Brazen it out, he decided. There were no witnesses and only her word against his. He could surely win that one. He might need a good solicitor; money was tight, his credit cards were maxed out. Damn the bitch.

Finally he decided to trust to luck and a sympathetic jury, if it came to it. He decided on a night in; keep away from the pub for a day or two until gossip died down. Di's threat, however, lurked in the back of his mind all that evening like a recurring nightmare.

Josie had an awful day. She had given the police her mobile number as they said they would need to contact her when the Crown Prosecution Service had made a decision about charging her. She found herself continually checking her phone and was on tenterhooks all morning. She had to take the bus into work as the police still had her car. She got there early and had time to re-rehearse her speech to Doug, her boss, as he wasn't due in until later. Whilst waiting for him she rang the solicitor Di had recommended, David Owens; his secretary said he could see her in her lunchtime. She wasn't looking forward to that.

Doug Fairview came into the open-plan office an hour later and called greetings to the half-a-dozen staff working at their desks. Josie took a deep breath and got up to follow him.

'May I have a word with you; please, Doug, as soon as possible?' Her voice was shaky.

'Can it wait a few minutes, Josie; I need to make a quick call?' He was putting his briefcase down and didn't look at her.

'It is urgent,' she persisted.

He looked at her and saw her distress. He nodded. 'Very well, come in and sit down. Shut the door.'

She sat in the chair opposite his and he lowered himself down on the other side of the desk.

'What's up?'

He was fond of Josie. She had worked for him for over three years and he had always found her polite, punctual and efficient. Lacking in enterprise, perhaps, maybe a bit mimsy, which was a word his wife used, a bit too meek as well, but a nice girl. Now he noticed her white face and strained look. He put his finger tips together and waited.

Slowly and falteringly Josie told him what had happened, leaving Mike's name out of it as she had to the police.

Doug sat in silence for a few moments when Josie had finished speaking. He was a kind man but he had not had experience of this sort of thing before. He wasn't sure what the correct procedure should be. Should she be suspended, sacked, counselled, what?

Finally he got up and went to his filing cabinet and took out a file with her name on it. He leafed through some papers before finding what he was looking for.

'It looks like you've got some annual leave still owing?' He raised an eyebrow at her.

'Yes,' Josie whispered.

'Right then, you take the rest of this week off and I'll mark it as leave. You keep in touch with me by telephone during the week to tell me what's happening and then next Monday we'll have a chat, either here or I can come to your home if you prefer. I shall have taken advice by then and will be able to tell you what will happen over your job. Is that clear?'

'Yes, thank you.' Josie got up to go.

'Meantime pass your current files on to Beverley and she can deal with them. I am so sorry, Josie, this is wretched and there's no point in saying anything else.' Doug also got up and putting his hand on her arm he steered her to the door. 'Let's hope this solicitor chap knows his onions and can get you out of this mess.' He opened the door.

'Thank you,' she said again and left.

She took another bus into the nearby town and walked as fast as she could from the bus station to the solicitor's office, only to find she was ten minutes early for her appointment. The receptionist asked her to sit in the waiting room. Thoughts and fears were buzzing in her head and she tried to pass the time by leafing through a magazine, but couldn't concentrate on the gossipy trivia that she would ordinarily have enjoyed. She hoped he wouldn't be long. She checked her phone again to see if the police had rung, but there was nothing.

David Owens was a large, fleshy man in his mid-fifties. He had an aura of capability and his eyes were shrewd and intelligent. He was wearing a rather shabby brown suit with a blue tie and a pale blue shirt. Every available surface in the office was piled high with files and there were a great many more spread across the floor. There were bookcases along all the walls and they, also, were bulging with books and papers. Josie had to pick her way carefully across the room to sit on the mahogany upright chair that he pulled out for her after shaking her hand.

'So,' he said, looking at a piece of paper in his hand as he also sat down. 'I see that I was recommended to you by Diana Pearson? Is that right?'

'Yes,' Josie replied.

'Fine; now I want you to tell me in your own words why you want my advice and then, if we agree that I act for you there will be formalities to go through and I'll explain the charges that may be incurred if we can't get legal aid. Do you understand?'

She nodded.

'Go on, then,' he said encouragingly and leant back in his chair fixing her with a kindly gaze.

Slowly, in a very quiet voice and barely looking at him, Josie recounted the events again. Again she omitted to mention what had happened at the flat. Several times David Owens stopped her and asked for clarification.

When she had finished Josie sat hunched in her chair looking at her hands, which she had laced together on her lap.

David Owens put his own hands on his desk and gently swung his swivel chair from side to side.

'You do realise,' he said gently 'that if I act for you I can only do so on the information you have given me and that I am duty bound to follow your instructions?'

Josie nodded.

'Therefore,' he went on, 'if there are things that happened that you are not telling me, things that might have a profound effect on the outcome of the case it is really important that you think very carefully. It would be much better for you if you told me everything now.' He raised his eyebrows at her in an encouraging way.

Josie glanced at him and then quickly fixed her gaze back on her own hands. It was tempting, very tempting, to tell this kind man about Mike. About what had happened in the flat and to tell him how frightened she had been and how stupid she was. She knew it would be a big relief. And yet, and yet...

Her indecision was obvious to the solicitor watching her. He didn't want to push her one way or another but time was moving on and he had another client to see and he also needed to speak to the Crown Prosecution Service and discover what they were going to do about charging Josie. He waited a few more seconds then leant forward prompting her into speech.

'No,' she whispered. 'That's all there is. It was my fault.' There was an air of resignation and finality about her bleak words.

Fifteen minutes later Josie was on her way home. David Owens had explained to her what would happen next. The Crown Prosecution Service would be charging her but in the meantime he would try and find out what section of the law they were going to use. She would then have to appear at the local Magistrates' Court in a few days' time. In due course the case would go before a judge at the Crown Court but if she pleaded guilty, as she appeared to indicate she would, there would not be a trial. He outlined possible sentences but told her she would be unlucky if a prison sentence were imposed. He told her again that if she had any mitigation she should tell him. She could ring him any time. Did she understand?

She said she did. They shook hands and she left.

Chapter 12

DURING THE NEXT FEW DAYS Mike's immediate concerns centred round whether Di had carried out her threat to tell the police of his involvement in the accident or not.

So far the police had not contacted him and nor had Di made a return visit. He remained fairly confident that he could brazen out any accusations were they to be made, and if it came down to Josie's word against his, he was also confident of his ability to win the argument. She was spineless, anyway. He had forgotten that a week or so ago he had considered her worth seducing and that she had shown some guts in kicking him. Now he just thought of her as a frigid bitch, a regrettable incident, best forgotten if possible. Di, however, seemed more of a problem. She was formidable and he wasn't so sure of his chances if she made a strong stand against him. He would have to wait and see.

Overall it had been a disappointing week for him. His boss had hauled him in on Monday 'to discuss sales figures', as he put it. In fact he was in for a bollocking, not just because his results were worse than anyone else's, but also for his timekeeping, use of the fuel allowance and his unwillingness to work overtime, to mention just three further 'issues'. His boss gave him a warning and a clear indication that he was not a great asset to the company. Mike, unwisely, attempted to sweet-talk his way out of trouble but the boss was unreceptive and growled at him to leave the room and pull his socks up or face the consequences – very soon.

Having avoided the King's Arms for the best part of a week to let the Josie situation die down, Mike returned there after the warning to off-load his work problems onto his mates. He had hoped the accident wouldn't be mentioned. He was disappointed. The local paper that evening carried a piece about Josie being charged and although she wasn't named his mates had worked out where the accident had happened and quizzed Mike a bit too closely for his comfort. He tried in vain to remember if he had mentioned Josie's name when bragging about her the previous week; it was going to get really uncomfortable if he had and the press named her, as they were sure to do sooner or later.

When he finally returned to his flat, somewhat the worse for wear, he made a mental note to start job hunting, preferably somewhere far away; he would look online at the trade magazines that weekend. 'Fresh fields and pastures new,' he said to himself as he staggered, unwashed, into his unmade bed.

Chapter 13

J OSIE'S NEXT THREE DAYS IN PRISON were spent in the induction class. There was so much information to be assimilated that she felt continuously punch drunk. She tried to make notes but found she couldn't process the information; it was all so unfamiliar. Nothing made sense.

She didn't know what to do about money; clothes; toiletries; visits; post; punishments; rewards; the list was unending and the answers so often unintelligible. Acronyms were endlessly used and although explained, most of the women couldn't remember what they were from one session to the next.

There were numerous forms to fill in. Josie was asked to list her academic achievements and when she reluctantly admitted to three reasonable 'A' levels and a college qualification, the tutor looked at her in surprise.

'Oh,' she said on looking at Josie's completed form, 'I see; you obviously don't need to do Maths and English Level One, then.' She looked curiously at Josie as if to say 'Why on earth are you here if you have these qualifications?' Josie hung her head but didn't volunteer any further information.

The tutor sighed and made some notes. 'You'll need to fill in a Work Party Preference Form.' She turned to her folders stacked untidily on the table and shuffled through a lot of papers before finding the right form. 'Fill this in and I'll let you know tomorrow what work you will have to do. It will depend on what vacancies there are.'

All the new women, after they completed their induction, would have to work or spend their time in the Education Centre trying to achieve basic literary and numeracy qualifications. Josie felt a new wave of fear wash over her at the thought of having to work with unknown women in an unfamiliar job. She was only just getting used to the eleven other new inmates and realising that they were no threat to her.

Joyce had been sitting beside her in the classroom. 'Please, Jo, help me,' she had said plaintively under her breath so that the tutor couldn't hear. 'I don't know what to put.' She pushed her educational achievement form in front of Josie.

Josie hadn't obliged. 'You just have to answer the questions,' she whispered impatiently and pushed the form back again. Momentarily she felt a pang of guilt when she saw Joyce's disappointed glance, but she had justified her meanness by saying to herself that she didn't owe anything to anyone and everyone had to look after themselves in a place like this. Somehow she had to get through the next six months and it would be easiest, she reasoned, if she kept herself to herself. She had forgotten Joyce's staunch defence during the attack in the dining room. She didn't notice that Joyce left most of the questions unanswered.

The form handed to her by the tutor listed the jobs available within the prison. Josie saw 'Hair and Beauty Salon' at the top of the list. The thought of working in a beauty salon for six months was awful. She had always liked having her own hair done but doing someone else's was not an attractive idea. She looked further down. 'Call Centre', then in small print it said, 'selling insurance'. 'I couldn't do that' was her immediate response. Then 'Laundry', 'Workshop',

'Waste Management', 'Bicycle Workshop' and 'Kitchens'. Nothing appealed to her. Feeling deeply depressed she skipped to the bottom of the list. 'Gardens', it said. Her biro hovered down the list again in indecision. She returned to 'Gardens', and pondered the possible implications. Work outside. Winter weather, cold and wet, dirty hands and muddy boots. And yet... She wasn't an outdoor girl, she knew that. Her Dad had always said when she offered to help him with digging or pruning, 'No, no, Josie girl, you keep your hands clean and nice, your old Dad'll do the dirty work; you can make a me a nice cuppa when I've finished, with a piece of your special sponge cake.' Now, however, as she agonised, she thought maybe there was something to be said for being outside after all, even in November. Fresh air rather than the stale, smoky atmosphere of her house and room; a chance, perhaps, to be alone, think her own thoughts, not to be hassled by anyone, not to be bullied. There was a paragraph at the bottom of the form that said that prisoners could change jobs after a month if they were unhappy and providing there were vacancies in the departments they chose. Right, she thought, gardening it is. She ticked the relevant box and took the form back to the tutor who read it and looked at her in surprise.

'Are you sure?' she asked. She didn't think Josie looked like an outdoor person either.

Josie hesitated for a moment, she really wasn't at all sure and with the tutor querying her decision she was even less sure. Finally, with the tutor tutting impatiently, Josie said 'Yes'.

'You may be lucky, then, I think they are short of workers in the gardens.'

The twice-daily walk to the dining room for lunch and supper was still agony. Mostly she was able to mingle unobtrusively with the other women from her house, putting her head down and her anorak hood up. An easterly wind, shivering its way through the skeletal trees and sending swirling brown heaps of fallen leaves across the concrete pathways, ensured everyone hurried towards the relative warmth of the dining room. Queuing for her food, waiting vulnerably exposed, made her feel sick. She was hyper-vigilant; she always tried to be in the middle of her group and her anxiety continued until they had finished their meal and returned to Beech House where she was able to relax, to a degree, lying on her bed or sometimes chatting with Joyce if she was there, until their sessions began again. There was no repetition of the assault, though all the new women had to put up with occasional barbed or loaded comments from other inmates. Their weaknesses and insecurities were subtly picked at, their ignorance used as a tool to highlight their vulnerability.

Looking round the classroom on her second day Josie thought it could have been any classroom anywhere. There were the tables; the bank of computers lined up along one wall; filing cabinets; piles of papers; dirty windows and shabby paintwork. What was different, though, and she was beginning to notice what was going on around her as she slowly emerged from the shock of her new surroundings, were the pupils. No eager schoolchildren, no disillusioned adolescents or cynical college students, but grown women. Josie looked along the faces opposite her. There was Marie, West Indian, in her forties, hennaed hair falling round her pockmarked face, chewing her biro as she tried to complete her medical record form. Next to her was the youngest woman, Charlene, from Nottingham. She was only eighteen and therefore subject to different rules as she was classed as a young offender. The previous day she had cried continuously and no one was able to console her. It had been awful. The tutor tried reassurance, the chaplain arrived and also failed to calm her and so all the sessions were punctuated by her sobbing, which unsettled everyone. Today she was obviously feeling better and was making an attempt to complete her educational achievement form. Next to Charlene was Pauline, who was the oldest of the new intake of prisoners, proudly telling everyone that she was fifty-five and had ten grandchildren and five great-grandchildren. She had untidy grey hair strewn with ineffective hairgrips and a face that looked as if it had seen more action than a battle-hardened marine. She was dismissive of the men in her life. Josie listened, unbelievingly, to tales of domestic violence, of multiple partners, of children by these different men, most of them in prison too. It was another world. But Pauline was funny, she made them all laugh. Josie was puzzled, how could anyone laugh when they were shut up behind huge metal gates and razor wire?

'C'mon, Miss Prim and Proper,' Pauline said to Josie at lunchtime on the second day as the induction group sat at a table together. 'Tell us what yer did to get in here; did yer raid the Post Office, then, or rob a bank?' She looked round the table for encouragement. The others obliged and laughed uproariously; they all looked expectantly at Josie.

She blushed and looked down at her bowl of vegetable soup, hating the attention and not wanting to divulge anything personal. She would have liked to tell Pauline to mind her own business.

'C'mon, Jo,' said Joyce encouragingly. 'Tell 'em.'

Josie had never been called Jo in her life before; it was alien to her, but she hadn't liked to protest when Joyce first used the abbreviation. Maybe she could get used to it and it would divorce her from the real Josie and would help to differentiate this new life from her old one. If she was 'Jo' could she be a different person? Involuntarily she took a deep breath.

'I killed a man,' she paused for a second, still looking at her bowl whilst trying to work out how best to phrase the rest of her reply, but before she could resume Pauline interjected.

'Yer what? Yer never did an' all?' She looked impressed. 'So, how d'yer do that, then? Knife? Was it yer boyfriend, then?' She used her own knife, red with tomato sauce, to make a series of stabbing motions in the air nearly knocking her cup of tea over. The others laughed again but they were all looking at Josie, waiting for her to continue.

'No, no,' Josie said hurriedly, almost laughing despite herself at the incongruity of Pauline's suggestion. 'It was an accident, a road accident, I didn't mean to kill him, I didn't even know him.'

'Yer must be a crap driver, then,' Charlene said with her mouth full of pizza.

It seemed easiest to agree. 'Yes, I suppose so.' Josie pulled a face and hoped they would talk about something else.

Marie, unexpectedly, came to her rescue: 'So what do you guys know about sending letters out?' she asked.

The conversation moved onto letters and visits, to Josie's relief. Before she had arrived at Edgehill, Josie had never given prisons or prisoners a second thought. She had black and white ideas about crime and punishment. 'Lock them up and throw away the key' more or less summed up her views when she read in the papers or saw on television the details and descriptions of a particularly heinous crime. That there might be exonerating circumstances or genuine reasons for people to have fallen into a criminal lifestyle and then into prison was a completely new thought. But now, hearing her companions talk of their families and home lives she realised that black was not necessarily black and that she had been privileged, with parents who cared for her and with good schooling on offer, which it would seem was unusual. It clearly wasn't necessarily a matter of right or wrong that the other girls were here, right now, with her. They had never been offered choices.

She didn't want to get involved with these women but she couldn't avoid sitting with them at meal times, benefiting, perhaps, from their protection. Inexorably, she found she was being drawn into their circle, sharing with them the problems of her entirely unwelcome and unexpected incarceration. She realised that she was beginning to want their approval and their support in this unfamiliar and intimidating environment. She didn't think she wanted friendship, not yet anyway, and preferably not at all. After all they weren't at all the sort of people she wanted to be friends with, were they? It would be better, surely, to keep her head down and get through the six months as uninvolved with anyone else as possible? But it was extraordinary, too, that they seemed to be able to laugh at their situation, even if the humour was bawdy and made her cringe. For the first time since her arrival at Edgehill Josie thought that possibly, just possibly, she might survive until her release next May.

Chapter 14

So, you've completed three days of induction, then?'
'Yes,' Josie replied cautiously.

She had been called on the tannoy to meet her Offender Manager in the long low wooden building that flanked the concrete path by the visits centre. She had entered the outside door and had been confronted by a narrow corridor with lots of offices on either side. Not knowing where to go she knocked on the first office door and asked for Mrs Harrison.

'Third room on the left,' a pleasant-looking older lady said in answer to Josie's hesitant enquiry. 'Do you have an appointment?'

'Yes.'

'Go on, then.' She smiled encouragingly.

Mrs Sadie Harrison had looked closely at Josie as she entered the room. She had seen a timid, youngish woman who was stooping slightly and holding her hands together in front of her. Her face had an anxious expression and she didn't smile. Her fair hair was tied back in a ponytail and her large blue eyes were apprehensive. Sadie sighed inwardly, realising that lack of assertiveness might be a problem, which was, in some ways, more difficult to deal with than over-confidence. The likelihood of bullying by other prisoners sprang into Sadie's mind as she invited Josie to sit down.

'How have you found the induction, then?' Sadie pushed her glasses onto the top of her grey hair.

'There's an awful lot to take in,' Josie replied.

'Yes, that's certainly true. Have they explained what an Offender Manager is?'

'Sort of, I think.' Josie was hesitant.

'Well, I am here to guide you through your time at Edgehill; hopefully helping you to make best use of it, and then I will assist you in making the transition back outside again at the end of your sentence. We shall meet every few weeks. Does that make sense?'

'Yes, thank you.'

Sadie Harrison had worked for many years with the Probation Service and had an enviable no-nonsense approach to her clients. She was nearing fifty and was hoping for early retirement in a year or two if she could ensure her pension was adequate. She was looking forward to spending more time with her family and indulging in her passion for antiques. Her dream was to open a little antique shop in her local high street, specialising in old clocks. Now, however, she looked again at Josie and then glanced down at the forms on her cluttered desk.

'One of the things we have to do together,' she said briskly, 'is to consider Victim Awareness.'

Josie looked blankly at her.

Sadie put her glasses back on her nose and pushed her grey fringe out of her eyes with a weary gesture. Thank goodness tomorrow was Friday. 'What do you know about your victim?'

Josie shook her head. 'I don't know, not really, they didn't tell me much about him.'

'Name? Age? Address?'

'His name was Tomas Brodinski, I think. He was from Poland.'

'Josephine, have you given any thought since the accident to this man, his family and the devastation that you may have caused them?'

Josie felt demoralised. Tears welled up and she hastily brushed them away. She couldn't look at Mrs Harrison. Had she thought about him? She knew she had hardly given him a second thought as a person with a family, someone whose life and future she had cut short, someone with hopes and fears just like her. She had thought of him a great deal but only in relation to her own situation and that wasn't what Mrs Harrison was asking. Josie didn't want to think about him as a person, now or ever. She looked at her hands in her lap and didn't answer.

'He will, almost certainly, have family: he was someone's son, brother, husband, even possibly father. I see from your case notes that he was twenty-eight years old. By your silence I am assuming you have not made any effort to find out about him and whether there was anything you could do to ease his family's grief?'

'No,' Josie whispered.

'No, well, it would have been inappropriate to contact the family before you were sentenced but you have certainly had plenty of time to make enquiries to ensure you understand the consequences of the accident on his family. Do you know how long he had been in this country?'

'No.' Josie wiped her eyes again with the back of her hand.

'In your pre-sentence report written for the judge it clearly says that Victim Awareness would be comprehensively covered. Don't you remember that?'

Josie shook her head again.

'Right,' said Sadie. 'I shall make some enquiries myself

and we will continue this conversation when I have more information. Now we'll discuss how you can make yourself useful while you're here.' She leafed through more papers and selected one. Josie could see it was a copy of her educational achievement form.

'You have three 'A' levels, I see, and you graduated with an HND in town planning? Is that right?

'Yes.'

'Do you realise that most of the women here have no educational achievements whatsoever? What does that suggest that you could offer?'

'I don't know.' Josie sniffed and tried to make an effort as Mrs Harrison waited, still holding the form in her right hand. 'Do you mean helping them read and write?'

'Of course.' Sadie tried not to show her exasperation with this ineffectual girl. 'Helping them do their canteen forms, reading their letters for them, helping them to compose letters to their family – all those sorts of things would not only benefit the other women but would help you considerably, too, don't you see that?'

'Oh.' Slowly the implications of what Sadie was saying began to seep into Josie's mind. 'Giving back,' she supposed it was called. Maybe it was a good idea. She remembered cold-shouldering Joyce's request the day before to help her complete a form, and again briefly felt a pang of guilt. None of this, though, fitted in with her understanding of what prison would be like. She had thought that all she needed to do was keep her head down, stay out of trouble and just exist for the next six months until she was released. Now she was discovering that she was expected to work and even to give help to other prisoners. This was a totally new concept altogether and she wasn't sure she liked it. She struggled to concentrate on what Mrs Harrison was now saying.

'...if you make the effort, both socially and at work, you will find the time goes much faster and you will feel much better about yourself, as well as being a great help to the other girls. You see what I'm saying?'

'I think so.'

The conversation continued, in a rather one-sided way, with Sadie Harrison explaining about the 'pathways' and 'targets' that Josie needed to follow or achieve over the next months.

Finally she put her pen down. 'That'll do for today; I'll see you again in a fortnight and we'll carry on then. By the way, what do you want to be called? Josephine is a bit formal, isn't it?'

Josie hesitated a moment before replying, 'Jo would be fine.' Somehow in saying it she felt she had jumped a hurdle.

It was almost dark when Josie left the Offender Management office. She trailed desolately back towards her house. It didn't seem fair: she was in prison which was quite awful in itself and being locked up was surely enough of a punishment. Then there was the shame to bear when she went home – if she went home – that again was another hurdle to jump. Maybe she couldn't go back to her house and job, nothing had been settled when she received her sentence last Monday. Was it only four days ago? It seemed a lifetime since she had stood in the dock. Nor had Doug Fairview been clear whether he would keep her job open for her. Now, on top of imprisonment, she was expected to work and also to 'pay back', she thought that was what Mrs Harrison called it, by helping other prisoners. Then there was the ghastly decision to be made about Tomas Brodinski. How could she contact his family? What on earth would she say to them? What good would it do?

Self-pity settled on her as the all-enveloping grey November dusk settled on the wire-enclosed establishment. Other prisoners, heading for the relative comfort of their houses, passed her as she trudged across the campus. She supposed it must be nearly supper time and she hoped Joyce had waited for her if their house had already been called to eat.

As she entered Beech House she could hear the television in the association room blaring with some quiz show; the raucous screams of those watching rang down the corridor. Obviously there had been no supper call as yet. Josie, having collected her key from the admin room, let herself into her own room and collapsed onto her bed still wearing her anorak. She curled up in a ball and sobbed miserably.

The tannoy blared. Josie reluctantly sat up and blew her nose. Her eyes were red and her face blotchy but she was beyond caring. She didn't even want any supper but knew she had to sign in to say she was present, as failure to do so would incur some unknown punishment that might mean loss of privileges – not that she was aware of having any privileges, but it was better to play safe. She waited a few moments expecting Joyce to knock, but no one came. Slowly she got to her feet and went out into the passage. Other women were laughing and chatting as they left the building to go to the dining room; the outside door slammed behind them. Josie realised with dread that she would have to walk on her own unless she hurried and caught up with them. She gave a quick knock on Joyce's door but there was no reply.

Running to catch up with the others she almost cannoned into Michelle who was just leaving her own room.

'Watch it!' Michelle fell back against the wall. She scowled at Josie.

'Sorry. Are you all right? Josie put out a hand, but Michelle had regained her balance.

'Yeah, but be careful.'

'Do you know where Joyce is?'

'Haven't you heard?'

'Heard what?'

'Joyce has been nicked,'

'What d'you mean?'

'She's in the seg.'

Seeing Josie's look of incomprehension Michelle elaborated 'She's in the Segregation Unit, the "Care and Support Unit". The officers found some gear in her room this afternoon.'

By this time the two women were outside walking towards the path leading to the dining room. Josie tried to peer into Michelle's face but even with the security lights positioned along the wire fence radiating circles of orange light, she couldn't make out her expression.

'I don't understand.'

Michelle sighed resignedly. 'Security searched her room and found a wrap of heroin; she's been put in the nick pending adjudication.'

'Heroin? Where did she get it from?'

'Dunno.'

'Would I be allowed to see her?'

'Nope.'

They had reached the dining room and although Josie

had loads of questions to ask she thought it better to keep quiet and hope the information she wanted would be forthcoming in general conversation.

In due course she was partially enlightened. She already knew that Joyce was on what she called 'meds' and went every day to the healthcare suite to receive it. She hadn't realised that the 'meds' was the heroin substitute Methadone, to help wean her off her addiction. No one seemed to know how Joyce had got hold of the heroin found in her room. Perhaps it had been planted there in retaliation for something else? There was mention of another prisoner who had been working outside in the community that day and had been seen talking to Joyce. Perhaps she had brought something back into the prison and had asked Joyce to hide it for her. There was much speculation.

'What's it like in seg?' Josie looked at Michelle.

'Boring.'

'No telly,' someone else said.

'What will happen to her?' Josie asked fearfully.

'Up to the Gov,' Michelle said. 'There'll be adjudication, maybe tomorrow, and she may get a week in there. Depends on what she says and if Security have any more intel.' She shrugged her shoulders and the conversation drifted onto other topics.

Josie picked at her supper mostly in silence as she listened to the others talking. Then she found herself wondering about Joyce. Why would she want the heroin, let alone hide it for someone else, if indeed she had? Who was the other woman? Would Joyce get anything to eat? Would she be all right? What would happen if she was moved from Edgehill, as someone suggested might be the case? Against her will

Josie found herself feeling responsible for the younger woman. Why? Was it because Joyce had stuck up for her, or because they had arrived together in the same van and shared so much in the first two days? She didn't know, but a strange feeling came over her almost as if Joyce was her little sister and needed protection. When she returned to her room after supper carrying her breakfast package, she realised that for the last hour she hadn't thought about her own problems.

'Room check. Everyone out by their doors, please.' There was a loud shout down the corridor as the two duty prison officers did a head count before lock-up. Josie got off her bed and went to her door and opened it so that she could be ticked off the list. The two officers went up one side of the corridor and down the other passing Josie on their way back down.

'Excuse me,' she said tentatively to the woman officer whom she had seen once or twice and who had seemed friendly.

'Yes, what?'

'Will you be seeing Joyce Davies this evening?'

'In CSU?'

'Yes.'

'Why?'

'I wondered if you could give her a message?'

'I probably shouldn't, but what is it?'

'Just to tell her I hope she's all right.' Josie wanted to add a lot more but looking at the officer she decided against enlarging.

'I'll try and remember when I get there. Okay?'

'Thank you very much.'

'G'night.'

'Goodnight.' Josie watched the officers as they finished their check and then left by the main door, locking it behind them. She turned to go back into her room.

'Jo?' It was Sharon, the woman who had the room next to hers who had overheard the conversation with the officer.

'Yes?'

'Come in here a mo.' She opened her door wider, inviting Josie in.

Josie was apprehensive; she hadn't spoken much to Sharon, who had seemed to want to keep herself to herself. She inched into the room, keeping her back close to the door.

Sharon leaned across Josie and pushed the door shut. She took a cigarette from behind her ear and lit it with a plastic lighter. Josie waited whilst Sharon inhaled and then slowly blew a stream of smoke out of her mouth; it lazily wound its way up towards the filthy ceiling and seemed to hang, like a pall, above the two women.

'Yer wanna be careful, kiddo. Keep away from the drugs crowd if yer know what's good for yer. They're nothin' but trouble.'

Josie waited, there was obviously more to come. Sharon took another lengthy drag.

'Yer friends with Joyce aren't yer?'

Josie nodded.

'Well, maybe yer didn't know that Joyce's boyfriend is banged up with Deanna's.' Deanna was the woman who had possibly framed Joyce by asking her to hide the heroin in her room. 'Wayne, I think 'is name is, owes Deanna's boyfriend a truckload of dosh. This could be payback time, yer see. Don't get involved.'

Josie wasn't sure she did see but didn't want to betray her ignorance by saying so. She nodded her thanks to Sharon and made her escape. Back in her room she slumped on her bed and tried to make sense of what she had just heard.

Chapter 15

SATURDAY WAS A MISERABLE DAY FOR JOSIE. Most of the women in Beech House had visitors in the afternoon and there had been much excitement and anticipation followed by much disappointment when the visitors left again. Josie wasn't allowed visitors as all the relevant checks on her had not been implemented. In fact she didn't know anyone who might want to visit her. She had no close relations and she didn't think her work colleagues would want to come, nor did she think she would want them to, anyway. David Owens, her solicitor, had said he might need to visit to tie up some loose ends, but that wasn't likely to be for some time. She had been asked to give potential visitors' names to Security but had declined to do so. Later she had wondered if either Di or her boss, Doug Fairview, might come, but it was such a long way from Northwood and she didn't want to write and ask them. It seemed like begging. What would she say to them anyway?

She had sat in her room listlessly watching television during visiting time. There had been no news about Joyce except that the adjudication had been adjourned whilst officers ascertained whether she had in fact been 'set up', as she was maintaining. She was to remain in Segregation for the time being. Josie had puzzled over the drug situation that Sharon had outlined but decided that she would have to wait and talk to Joyce and see what she had to say. It was all very strange. She couldn't see how anyone could bring illicit substances into prison as everyone coming in from work, or as a visitor, was routinely searched and the sniffer dogs were often on duty too. She had seen them that day, two lovely brown and white spaniels on leads, with their handlers, on their way to the visits centre.

On Sunday morning Josie took some of her clothes to the house laundry room, hoping that there might be a free washing machine she could use. Sharon was there ironing a pair of jeans.

She gave Josie a long look before asking 'Yer all right?'

'Yes, thank you,' Josie replied, stuffing her clothes into the vacant machine and turning the dial to start it. She didn't look at Sharon.

'I'm going to the chapel in a bit, d'yer wanna come with me?'

Josie looked up, surprised.

'They don't shove religion down yer, if that's what yer wondering.' Sharon almost smiled. 'It passes the time; Sundays can be very long days. Service'll be well over before dinnertime.'

One of the chaplains had visited the new women in induction but Josie had forgotten about it. Maybe going to the chapel would pass the time.

'Thanks, if you don't mind me coming with you.'

'Wouldn't have asked if I did. Be ready in half an hour,' Sharon said, looking at her watch.

Josie had mixed feelings about going with Sharon to the service. Church had never been her thing, though her Mum had sometimes gone to the Methodist chapel in the village and Josie herself had joined a youth group at the C of E church, which had been quite fun. She'd even been confirmed, as that was what her friends were doing at the time, but then she didn't like the new vicar so she had stopped going. Apart from an occasional wedding and a couple of carol services she had not been inside a church for over ten years.

The chapel was light and airy; there were vases of artificial flowers dotted around and banners hanging on the walls. The altar was decked with vivid red artificial poppies and Josie realised with surprise that it was Remembrance Sunday. She had forgotten that British Legion sellers had been traipsing the streets of Northwood a week ago and that there had been a tray of poppies on the reception desk at her office. She had put in a pound and had pinned the poppy to the blue jacket she often wore for work. The jacket and the poppy would now be gathering dust on the back of the chair in her bedroom, a forlorn reminder of the atrocities of war and of her old abandoned life.

There was a gaggle of prisoners already seated on a curving row of wooden chairs facing the altar. Sharon and Josie sat on the end of the row behind. A few officers sat behind them and occasionally their radio sets crackled with announcements but the officiating minister ignored all interruptions and extended a warm welcome to everyone. A prisoner played the piano, quite well, Josie thought. To her surprise she enjoyed singing the hymns, some of which she knew despite the long years since she had last sung them. The minister gave a short address about peace and reconciliation. At the end of the service the two minutes' silence was observed. The minister shook her hand as she and Sharon were leaving.

'You're new, aren't you? Don't I remember seeing you in induction last week?' She held onto Josie's hand and smiled in a friendly manner

'Yes.'

'Well, it's good to see you here with Sharon, you must come again. You can pop in any time, you know, the door is always open.' She paused a moment to say goodbye to someone else, but still retained Josie's hand. She turned back to her. 'I think I heard you sing rather well, didn't I? How about joining the choir? We've just started to practise for the Christmas Carol Service and some new voices would be good.' She smiled encouragingly at Josie. 'Talk to Sharon about it and let me know. We practise on Tuesdays before supper.' She gave Josie's hand a final squeeze.

Chapter 16

AUTUMN HAD SLIPPED quietly into winter. Fog and sleet took turns to dress the prison campus in equally dreary shades of grey during November. Long-fallen leaves became rain-sodden and black as the prisoners' feet trampled them into pulp on their daily walks across the campus. Dead twigs and bigger branches were storm-tossed onto the paths and flowerbeds, discarded by the trees as if sloughed off like dead skin.

For Josie, the reminder by Mrs Harrison of the man she had killed brought death uncomfortably close. For the last few months she had subconsciously blotted out the incontrovertible evidence of what she had done to Tomas Brodinski and his family; now she realised she had to face the fact that he had been a sentient human being and not just an uncomfortable traffic accident statistic. It was so painful reliving that ghastly evening in July; blotting it out seemed an easier option, but one that she was now being denied.

Josie was regretting her decision to work in the gardens even before she had started. She walked along the puddle-strewn paths early on a Monday morning to meet her supervisor in the old stable block where he had his office, wishing she had chosen work that could have meant staying indoors in the relative warmth, perhaps in the laundry or even the much-despised beauty salon. She was feeling the cold already; her anorak wasn't great quality; it hadn't needed to be when she had only had to wear it previously to bridge a few minutes' walk from her warm car to her even warmer office. She didn't have any gloves or a scarf. It was only thanks to David Owens that she had the anorak and a pair of thick trousers to wear. At the last meeting she had with him before her court appearance he had gently suggested that she pack a small bag to bring with her, just in case, he had said. She had asked why, and he had reminded her that the judge had the option to send her to prison, and, even though it was unlikely, she wouldn't have any opportunity of going back home to collect stuff if that is what happened. She had asked him what to put in the bag. He had said think of it as an overnight case but had added that a warm coat, trousers and jersey would be a good idea, likewise writing things and a book or two. But she was not to put in a mobile phone or any computerised device. Categorically not, he said.

She met three or four women coming out of the gardening office as she arrived; they were wearing green overalls and wellington boots. The first woman eyed Josie.

'Hey girls, look, a new recruit. Yer'll be unblocking drains this morning; it's what everyone has to do their first day, and without gloves!' She laughed unkindly and the others sniggered as they sauntered down the path.

A man came to the door and called after the group.

'That's enough, Sarah. Report to me at break-time. I won't have that kind of behaviour as you very well know.' He turned to Josie and held the door open for her.

'Ignore them, they'll be doing it themselves if there's any more cheek.'

There was another group of women waiting in the office. 'Off you go,' he said to them. 'And don't forget the admin block. The No 1 Governor has important visitors today and he wants the paths swept sharpish. Don't forget to take the wheelbarrow this time, either.'

The women left and the man looked at Josie.

'Good morning. You are ...' he moved to his desk and looked at a list 'Ah yes, Josephine Anderson?'

'Yes.'

'Well, Josephine, have you any gardening experience?'

'Only a bit,' she admitted.

'No matter. Find some overalls from the hooks over there and put them on.' He waved a hand towards the wall near the door where there were several green overalls hanging up like the ones Josie had seen the other women wearing. 'You'll find wellies just outside the door, hopefully a pair will fit you; bring more socks next time if they're too big.'

Josie did as she was told.

'Gloves are over there,' he said pointing to a shelf, 'despite what Miss Clever Clogs said to you just now, gloves will be worn.' He smiled broadly and Josie found herself relaxing a bit. 'Now you need to sign this if I am to let you loose with secateurs this morning.' He handed her a form and a biro and pointed to a column on the sheet. 'Sign there. You'll have to sign them in again at the end of the session.'

She signed and then looked up at him enquiringly.

'Okay, then, thanks.' He took back the form and biro and put them on his desk. 'Now I want you to go and find Amy who's working on the bed behind that polytunnel.' He pointed out of the window. 'She's taking out the old runner bean plants. Frost's got them now and they need cutting down and putting on the compost heap. She'll show you what to do. This afternoon you can dig the plot over. Off you go.' He handed her the pair of secateurs and nodded at the door.

Josie heard Amy before she found her. She was singing loudly as she bent over a wheelbarrow chopping blackened runner bean stems into compostable size. On seeing Josie approach Amy stood up and waved a hand in greeting. She broke off from her song.

'Hi, I'm Amy; I'm from Jamaica where it's a whole lot warmer than here. Who are you?'

'I'm Jo.'

'Can yous sing, Jo?' was Amy's next question as Josie reached her.

How odd, Josie thought, twice in the last two days I have been asked about singing. 'It depends what it is,' she replied cautiously.

'Stuff from the shows, soul, gospel, hymns, anything you like.' Amy grinned, showing big gaps in her front bottom teeth and a gold tooth prominent at the top. She launched into 'Amazing Grace' and Josie, almost in spite herself, joined in. They reached the end, more or less together.

'We'll get this lot shifted in no time. Mr P won't know what's hit him.' Amy laughed happily. 'C'mon then,' and she showed Josie how to cut the old bean stalks off close to the bottom of the plant and then chop the stems in pieces before shoving them into the wheelbarrow.

'Leave the roots in the soil, they've got lots of nitrogen in them,' she ordered. 'Good for next year's crop.' Then she started to sing 'Row the Boat'.

After three songs of Amy's choosing Josie put her hand up. 'My choice now,' she said, and, almost without thinking, she launched into a piece from *The Mikado*:

'To sit in solemn silence in a dull, dark dock
In a pestilential prison with a life-long lock,

Awaiting the sensation of a short, sharp shock
From a cheap and chippy chopper on a big black block.'

Amy, a grin of delight spreading across her face, tapped in rhythm with her secateurs on the handle of the wheelbarrow. Her hoop earrings swung jauntily from side to side.

'Cool, man,' she said approvingly as Josie finished. 'Go on, sing it again!'

Josie did so and then they both doubled up with laughter. It was the first time since the last night of the show, way back in July, that she had recited any of the words or sung any of the songs from *The Mikado* and somehow it felt as if a barrier had been broken. It was good to make Amy laugh, too, even if she was totally ignorant of Josie's involvement with the song. Before Amy could ask any difficult questions Josie started, rather more tentatively, on 'Praise my Soul the King of Heaven', which they had sung in chapel the previous day.

Chapter 17

AT THE END OF HER FIRST DAY working in the gardens Josie walked slowly back to Beech House. It was twilight and the glow from the security lights spread orange pools along the path. She watched her shadow, short and fat when she was in the centre of the pool of light and then gradually elongating as she moved to the perimeter. She remembered as a child trying to surprise the shadow and jump away from it, to fool it into thinking she was someone else and then to ambush it again. She would run along the pavement to the next street light and repeat the exercise all the way home from school on dark afternoons. Now she was too tired to hurry, or to jump out of the light like her younger self; her legs ached and her back ached and she longed for a shower. To her surprise it hadn't been a bad day. It had been all right working with Amy. Josie had never met anyone like her before, and they had completed all the work that Mr P had asked them to do. It had been satisfying and she had felt pleased when he had congratulated them.

'Well done, you two. See you tomorrow,' he had said and she found herself smiling at him and Amy as she left.

Her thoughts were interrupted by a lone blackbird, his cover drawn, who flew from the laurel hedge adjacent to the path and 'chuk chukked' his disapproval at her as she passed. She watched him for a moment as he settled noisily in a hawthorn tree and perched, a black silhouette among the leafless twigs. She felt guilty at disturbing him and hoped he would return to his roosting place before nightfall. Seeing him made her think of her blackbird family at home; she wondered if her neighbour was feeding them.

There was the usual noise of televisions when she reached Beech House as most of the women were back from work and were relaxing until called for supper. Doors were open and there was laughter from the association room where a group of prisoners were, as usual, watching a raucous game show.

She reached her room and was about to unlock the door when she noticed Joyce's door was ajar and a light was shining out onto the passage. Josie knocked and pushed the door wider open. Joyce was sitting on her bed with her back to Josie. She didn't look up.

'Hi, Joyce? You okay?' Josie asked.

There was no reply so Josie crossed to the bed and faced Joyce. Her face was screwed up and tears rolled down her cheeks.

'What's wrong?'

Joyce shook her head.

'Come on.' Josie sat beside her. 'You've been let out, that must be good, surely?'

'Yea, no. it's not me, it's Wayne.' Joyce sniffed loudly and mopped her eyes with a rather grubby tissue.

'What do you mean?'

Falteringly and inarticulately Joyce tried to explain. Josie had difficulty understanding all the implications but she grasped various salient facts despite much sniffing and sobbing. Yes, Deanna's step-dad had visited and given her the heroin for her own use. Yes, Deanna had given the heroin to Joyce as she was expecting a room search, and yes, Joyce had hidden the heroin in her room because Deanna had threatened her that if she didn't her boyfriend would beat up Joyce's boyfriend, Wayne, and frame him for other drug-related offences that would be likely to vastly increase his time in prison. Deanna would also ensure that Joyce lost her privileges at Edgehill and would be bullied and beaten up by Deanna's cronies if she didn't comply. It seemed very dramatic to Josie but clearly Joyce was terrified.

'Did you tell the Gov you've been framed?' Josie asked.

'Nah, yeah, sort of, but I'm scared of what Deanna'll do if I split on her.'

'Have you split on her?'

'Nah.'

'Have they punished you, then?'

'Yeah. No telly and no visits for six weeks. I won't get to see me Mam, she was coming next week. I might as well give up now, I know this'll go on and on. Deanna won't let go.' Joyce was becoming distraught.

'You can't give up.' Josie sounded more positive than she felt.

'Wanna bet? I've tried before. I'll do it proper this time.' Joyce pushed back the left sleeve of her shabby grey jersey.

Josie looked at Joyce's arm. Criss-crossed from wrist to elbow were scars, some old and dried up, others relatively new, still red with raised edges; some were still suppurating. As she watched in disbelief, not fully understanding what she was seeing, Joyce got up and took a step towards the table where her television had sat until it had been removed. She opened the drawer and pulled something out. For a second the dingy light shone on a piece of metal in Joyce's right hand then, with a lightening movement, she slashed at her arm and Josie, rooted to the spot, watched in terror as globules of blood dripped on to the floor. Each globule caught the light and shone as it splashed onto the dirty linoleum creating little dark red pools of desperation. Josie, on her feet now, stood immobile as the blood dripped remorselessly down; she looked at Joyce's face and saw a strange expression of relief and triumph mixed together. Joyce wasn't looking at her and seemed oblivious of her presence.

Suddenly Josie came to her senses. 'No, don't. Stop, oh please stop.' She shouted, and reached out to take the razor blade.

Joyce emerged from her near trance at the shout.

'Keep away, Jo.' She spat the words. 'I'll slash yer, too, if yer come closer.' She wielded the blade in front of Josie's face and Josie was in no doubt that she would do what she was threatening.

Panicked, feeling sick and with a black mist swirling round her head, Josie turned to the door, trying frantically to remember what she had been told to do if there was an emergency. 'Panic button, where's the panic button?' She knew that Beech House was probably empty, everyone having gone to supper, so it was up to her to get help. She stumbled into the passage and looked up and down in desperation. To her left on the wall beyond Sharon's room she saw the red button. She launched herself at it and thumped it as hard as she could with her fist and then sank to the ground, sliding to the floor with her back to the wall and ending up sitting with her head on her knees and her hands covering her ears as the raucous sound of the alarm shattered the silence. She had no idea how long she waited before the outside door was pushed violently open and three officers raced up the passage to her. It had probably been a few seconds at most, she realised later.

'Which room?' the first officer shouted at her.

Josie gestured at Joyce's door, unable to speak. They rushed past her and into the room. More officers quickly joined them and Josie was aware of radio messages crackling from the room summoning healthcare and an ambulance. No one took any notice of her and she remained slumped on the floor of the passage until everything had gone quiet and she had watched Joyce being stretchered out into the dark, cold night. She had no idea if she was alive or dead.

The whole prison would have known from the alarm that there had been 'an incident' as they called it, so when the Beech House women returned from supper a few minutes after Joyce had gone and saw Josie still sitting on the floor in the passage, they realised she had been party to it – whatever 'it' was. Sharon and Michelle knelt beside her. Josie was inarticulate; all she could say was 'Joyce'. It didn't take long for them to put two and two together after seeing Joyce's empty room and pools of blood still visible on the floor. Josie was helped up and taken to the association room, a blanket was wrapped round her and a hot, sweet cup of tea put in her hands. Sharon sent another prisoner to the dining room with instructions to ask the officers to allow her to bring back sandwiches for Josie as she had missed supper. The television was turned on and soon the association room was full of concerned women watching an old episode of 'Neighbours' as a cover for keeping an eye on Josie.

One of the younger women came in and saw Josie sitting with her tear-blotched face. 'What's the matter with Miss Hoity Toity, then?' she jeered.

Sharon turned on her. 'Apologise this minnit,' she ordered. 'Don't yer dare speak to Jo like that.'

The girl looked shamefaced. 'Sorry, Jo.' She said meekly. 'What's happened, then?' she turned to the others.

'Joyce's tried to top 'erself.'

'Oh my God. That's awful. Is she okay?'

'Dunno yet. They may have taken her to hospital or maybe put her in the constant watch suite if she's not too bad,' Michelle said.

The Beech House girls waited anxiously until the officers arrived to lock up for the night. They learned that Joyce had been taken to hospital. No one could tell them anything else so it was a subdued and worried group of prisoners who huddled together for company and reassurance in the association room that evening. Josie, still shocked and dazed by what had happened, nonetheless felt more at ease with the other women than she had before. The warmth and sympathy they showed her, the solidarity and concern, was a new experience for her.

Chapter 18

'I THINK I'LL GO and see Josie,' Di said. It was Saturday morning nearly three weeks after Josie had been sentenced. Di and Peter were just finishing breakfast.

'Really?' Peter was surprised. 'I thought you were going to write to her, wouldn't that do?' He took another piece of toast and spread a liberal amount of butter on it.

'No, I've been thinking. Letters'll get opened and I don't like the idea of what I write being scrutinised by some prison officer. I know she hasn't any relations, not close ones, anyway. So she must be pretty miserable. Maybe a visit would cheer her up. I don't think anyone else will go.' Di picked up her plate and coffee mug and took them to the dishwasher.

'When are you thinking of going?'

'Not sure. I don't know when visitors are allowed. I'll have to ring the prison or maybe the website would tell me. A Saturday would be best.' She absentmindedly reorganised the top layer of the dishwasher.

'D'you want me to drive you? It's quite a long way.'

'That's kind, but you wouldn't want to see her and you know you hate waiting. I'll be okay, thanks. You could work out the route though.'

'I'll do that. By the way did you ever find out what Mike is up to?' Peter folded his napkin and slid it into the silver ring with his initials on. 'Josie might be reassured if he really has left the area. Easier for her to come back when she's let out, I would have thought.'

'I think he's gone, heaven knows where. I must ask around and see if anyone does know for certain. It would make a big difference if he has really moved away. Good riddance and all that.' Di wiped the draining board with a dishcloth as if she were washing away the most disgusting of smells. 'I still wish I'd told the police about him, you know.' She rung out the dishcloth and placed it tidily on the washing up bowl.

'No.' Peter was emphatic. 'You were right not to interfere any more than you did.'

Di sighed. 'Maybe.'

Later she checked the Edgehill website and discovered that Saturdays were visiting days but that she had to contact the prison well in advance if she wanted to go, as she needed a visitors' pass. Then she made a few telephone calls to see if she could find out about Mike. No one was sure if he had left the area or not so she drove round to his flat. There was no reply when she rang his bell and tellingly there was a 'To Let' sign up outside the building.

As she was getting back into her car a woman came out of the communal door.

'Can I help you?' she asked. 'I saw you from the window, who do you want?'

'Thanks,' Di said. 'I was looking for Mike Williams, does he still live here?'

'No, thank goodness,' the woman said with some vehemence. 'He left about two weeks ago. I don't know where he went. Didn't leave a forwarding address, I gather, but the agent might know.' She gestured at the 'To Let' sign. 'Towards Bristol, someone said.'

'Thank you very much.' Di smiled at the woman and got back into her car. 'Toe-rag,' she said to herself, 'he must have waited to see what happened to Josie in court and then shoved off as fast as he could. Hope he rots in hell.'

She drove home and then emailed the prison to see when she could visit.

Chapter 19

THREE WEEKS LATER, on a Saturday morning, Di drove
to Edgehill. She wasn't looking forward to visiting
Josie, not because of Josie herself, but because it would be a
completely unknown environment, way outside her comfort
zone. She was annoyed with herself for being apprehensive.

She reached Edgehill soon after one o'clock. Other
cars were arriving and disgorging their passengers into the
wire-fenced visitors' car park. Di looked with curiosity at
the people getting out, then thought she should be more
circumspect and not be seen to take too keen an interest, so
she lowered her gaze and took especial care to lock her car
securely and leave her mobile phone and most of her cash
in the glove box, which she also locked. The prison had
stipulated exactly what she could and could not bring inside.

There was a large man getting out of a BMW parked next
to her car. He was dressed entirely in black; he had shiny,
pointy black shoes and a coat with a velvet collar and she
thought she could see tattoos showing between his lengthy
hairline and his coat collar. She avoided meeting his eyes
when he glanced speculatively at her but she couldn't help
imagining how he earned his living and wished Peter had
been with her so that they could giggle together. It was
actually quite intimidating coming on her own; she hadn't
realised that it would be, and now, belatedly, she wished
she had accepted Peter's offer to accompany her.

'Too late,' she said to herself and took a deep breath.
'Come on, old girl, you can do this, you know you can.'

She followed other people out of the car park and into a visitors' waiting room where prison officers patted her down, scrutinised her paperwork and checked the contents of her handbag. There were prominent notices all around warning what would happen if visitors attempted to bring illicit substances into the prison and there was an amnesty box fixed to the wall. Di didn't see anyone put anything into it. She perched a little nervously on a white plastic chair and waited with everyone else. From her chair she could see the security fencing topped with razor wire that surrounded the prison; it was a stark reminder of the clientele living inside. It seemed incongruous to Di that Josie, meek, timid Josie, was now incarcerated with thieves, murderers and drug addicts in a place like this. She looked at the other people waiting; older women with harassed, careworn faces trying ineffectually to control their grandchildren; younger men and women probably visiting their mothers, and men, partners or husbands, most of whom kept popping into the chilly outdoors for a quick cigarette, who looked as if they would rather have been anywhere than here. Poor people, Di thought, what a ghastly mess their lives must be.

Soon after one-thirty the officers began to chaperone the visitors into the prison in groups of ten. Di was in the third group. They followed an officer through two sets of enormous metal gates, waiting between the gates for one set to shut before the next could open, herded like cattle Di thought, and then chided herself for being so unimaginative.

The group straggled along after the officer until he reached a low building and unlocked its double doors. They entered and were shown by other officers where to sit. Di was escorted to a small table that had a chair on

117

either side, and told to wait. She looked around: there was a tea bar along one wall with two prisoners busily serving visitors with plastic cups of tea and coffee. There was a range of sandwiches and cakes for sale and squash for the children. It seemed to be doing good business. Some prisoners were already sitting with their visitors and the buzz of conversation gradually rose as more people arrived. It could have been a reception area in any hospital or airport, Di thought, except for the presence of the officers with their endlessly clanging keys and watchful eyes.

Prisoners arrived in dribs and drabs through a door at the far end of the room from where Di sat. She watched the door being opened and closed by an officer as the women came in; she watched their faces; some evidently excited, some fearful, some sulky and apparently uninterested. Di wondered what was behind their demeanour. Were some of them new prisoners ecstatic at seeing their families again? Were they 'old lags' with nothing much to say, knowing they still had years to serve? Did they have guilty consciences over the difficulties their partners had to deal with at home? Housing problems, errant children, mounting debts, betrayals; and that might just be for starters? She saw the tattoo man from the car park sitting with a young blonde woman. He seemed to be doing all the talking and the woman appeared submissive. I wonder what the relationship is, thought Di.

Her thoughts were interrupted when a quiet voice said 'Hello, Di.'

Josie was standing beside her.

Di jumped up and gave her a hug. 'Josie, how are you?'

'I'm fine.'

They both sat down and Di looked at the woman opposite her. Josie was thinner, her hair was longer than Di remembered and it was tied neatly back with a faded blue ribbon. She wasn't wearing any make-up and seemed pale and drawn but there was an air of self-control and stillness about her that seemed different from the old Josie. She was wearing a dark blue jersey, a pair of brown corduroy trousers and scuffed white trainers.

'Well, then,' Di said. 'It's good to see you.'

'It's good to see you, too, thank you for coming. How was the journey?'

'Not bad, traffic was reasonably quiet, being Saturday. But tell me about you; are you really all right and are you treated okay?'

Josie gave a half smile. 'I'm fine and it's not too bad overall.' She looked down at her hands.

Somehow, Di thought, I need to break through the stiffness and find out what's really going on. She tried another tack.

'There's a big age range of women here, isn't there?' She looked round the room at the assembled prisoners.

'Yes, from eighteen upwards, and I think we have about a dozen women over sixty.'

'Goodness,' Di exclaimed. 'The website said there was a real emphasis on work and rehabilitation. Do you have to work?'

'I work in the gardens.'

Di raised her eyebrows; it wasn't what she expected. 'Is that what you wanted to do, or were you just told to do it?'

'It was my choice.'

Slowly and with much prompting from Di, Josie expanded on her life in prison. She described her room and Beech House, the dining room, the food and the daily routine. She began to relax. Di asked about friends and whether she had any.

Josie was silent for a moment.

'You know,' she said hesitantly, 'I didn't really have close friends before I came here. I didn't think I needed them. I got on well with my work colleagues but we didn't socialise. I was quite happy at home, even after Dad died, just pottering along. There was the operatic society once a week and all the other usual routines. Having close friends didn't seem important. I thought when I came here that I would just keep my head down, avoid other people, do what I was told, make no fuss and wait for the time to pass. You know?' She smiled ruefully.

'But it hasn't worked out like that?'

'No. I suppose it was inevitable that I would be picked on a bit, even bullied, when I arrived. Some of the other women called me Miss Hoity Toity,' she smiled again, wryly. 'I can understand why, though it hurt. There were other things, too.' She paused, remembered the trip-up in the dining room on her first day. 'But I found people stuck up for me, even though they didn't know me; there's a real sense of fair play and whenever someone is upset, for whatever reason, most of the other girls are so friendly and kind. It's very humbling, really, as many of them have so little and I have so much.'

'What do you mean?'

'Well, I had always taken for granted that I had loving parents who wanted the best for me. I had a nice home and good schooling and job opportunities. Most of our girls here have never had any of that. Probably never will. Apart from anything else so many of them are in abusive relationships.' She paused and looked at Di as if to see if she understood. Di nodded encouragingly. 'I work in the gardens with a girl called Amy. She's from Jamaica and was acting as a drug mule for her boyfriend when she was arrested. It was really his fault, but he's not in prison. She's got years to serve but she's always cheerful. She loves singing and now she's got me in the chapel choir too and we're singing a duet in the carol service next week.'

Di was impressed. 'So are you saying that Amy has become your friend?'

'Yes, but not just Amy, there's Joyce and Sharon, too. We look out for each other.'

'What happens over Christmas? Are lots of people allowed out?'

'Some are, but most of us stay here. I think we have a special meal and some entertainment. There's a competition for the best-decorated house, too, and we're busy making stuff for that. They say some people get very upset, which is not surprising, I suppose. It must be very difficult if you've got kids and you can't be with them at Christmas.'

They chatted some more. Then an officer called out last orders for the tea bar and Di realised she would soon have to leave.

'I thought you might like to know that Mike has moved from Northwood.' She kept her tone light and avoided eye contact with Josie as she spoke.

Josie flinched slightly but said nothing.

'We think he's gone to the Bristol area,' Di continued. 'I thought you'd want to know; it might make it easier for you to come home knowing he's not around.'

'Thank you for telling me.' Josie's eyes were narrowed into slits and her mouth pursed into a thin line. She looked away.

Di wished she had not mentioned him; Josie's reaction was so unexpected. She changed the subject.

'Is there anything I can do for you at home?' she asked. 'Do you have everything you need here?'

Josie refocused and shook her head. 'David Owens arranged for an agent to see to everything to do with the house, so it should be all right. We can buy stuff here from a catalogue if we want, but I don't need much, thank you.'

Prison officers were chivvying the visitors to leave so Di stood up. 'Would you like me to come again in a few weeks' time?' she asked, picking up her handbag.

Josie got to her feet as well. Officers were escorting the prisoners out and she knew she had to go too. 'It would be very nice,' she said politely, 'if you have the time to spare.'

'I'll come then, but write to me if you need anything. Happy Christmas, when it comes.' She gave Josie another hug and followed the waiting officer. She turned at the door to wave goodbye but Josie had already left.

Di's journey home seemed shorter than on the way to Edgehill and she was glad that there was nearly an hour of daylight left to help her. Her preconceived ideas about what it would be like to visit a prison and about the prisoners themselves hadn't really materialised. Yes, it was grim seeing the wire and the big gates; it was intimidating hearing the endless chinking of keys and the clanging of locks being opened and shut; it was uncomfortable knowing that she, too, was locked in for the duration of her visit and couldn't have got out unassisted even if she had wanted to. Despite these negative aspects she had found the visiting room cheerful and well decorated, the officers were polite and helpful and the prisoners didn't look browbeaten and they seemed to react positively to the officers when asked to do something. It was rather surprising.

She said all this to Peter when she reached home. She sat at the kitchen table and he poured her a large glass of red wine.

'Drink that and tell me about Josie.' He returned to the cooker and carried on stirring a saucepan of Bolognese. 'Did you tell her about Mike?'

Di took a welcome mouthful of wine. 'Mm, but it was odd.'

'Why?'

'She looked really angry and turned her head away without saying anything. I thought she would be pleased to hear he had gone.'

'Unfinished business, I suppose, and a reminder, as if she needed it, of what an idiot she had been.'

'Maybe you're right. I didn't like to ask her what her plans are when she gets let out, there's still quite a time to go; I suppose I can find out when I go next time.'

'You're going again?' Peter was surprised. 'You're a glutton for punishment, I must say.'

Di laughed. 'It wasn't nearly as bad as I was expecting and it's obvious she doesn't have anyone else going. I'll wait till the New Year anyway and then I'll see.'

Chapter 20

JOSIE, AFTER BEING SEARCHED by the officers, made her way slowly back to Beech House. Other women passed her, laughing and chatting about their visitors. Josie envied them their equanimity. She was feeling very unsettled; seeing Di had been more difficult than she had anticipated. Like a flashback to a life she had almost forgotten and wasn't sure she wanted to remember. She passed the flower beds that she and Amy had been working on the day before. They had cleared leaves, weeded, cut back shrubs and then helped Mr P spread new compost over everything. He had pointed out a lovely-smelling shrub, Viburnum Bodnantense, he had called it, and she and Amy had stopped to sniff the tiny pink whorls of flowers on their bare, angular twigs. It was the most heavenly scent and she had remembered that her neighbour at home had the same shrub overhanging the dividing fence. The scent had provoked poignant memories yesterday and now Di had done the same today. It seemed too much to bear. She was glad to reach her room and was about to enter when Joyce called out to her from next door.

'Jo, come in 'ere.'

Joyce had been kept in hospital for twenty-four hours after slashing her wrist. She had then been under constant supervision in case she tried to do the same thing again. Now, however, she was free to come and go but because of her earlier misdemeanour with Deanna's drugs, was not yet allowed visitors, nor to have her television back. She was sitting on her bed looking at a magazine.

'Did yer visitor come, then?' she asked as Josie appeared, somewhat reluctantly, in the doorway.

Josie nodded, 'Yes, she did.'

'Go on then, what did she say?'

'We talked about what it's like being in here and then we talked a bit about home.' Josie sat on the edge of Joyce's bed. 'It was funny, I really found I didn't want to know what's going on back there, I don't know why, maybe it's because there's still such a long time to wait till I can go back.' She didn't want to admit to herself or to Joyce that talking about Mike had been too difficult and had brought back too many agonising feelings. 'Did you ring your Mum?'

'Yeah, but we got cut off. I think my card's run out. She did say that Wayne's in a lot of trouble and may get more time added on.'

Joyce looked so miserable that Josie put an arm round her. 'Maybe it'll be for the best, you know, that you don't see him. Perhaps you should start to think about a life without Wayne – he's hardly done you any favours, has he?' She squeezed Joyce's shoulder and wondered if she hadn't been a bit too intrusive. She was surprised at herself for doing the agony aunt thing; previously she wouldn't have got involved or even had an opinion.

'I dunno,' Joyce sniffed and wiped her nose on her sleeve. 'That's what me probation officer said before I came in but I don't know any other sort of life, do I, without Wayne and me Mam?'

Josie knew there wasn't an easy answer to the question. She got up. 'Come on, it's got to be supper time, did you hear them call?'

'No, not yet,' Joyce hesitated as if trying to pluck up

courage. She looked up at Josie with pleading brown eyes. 'Jo, will you 'elp me?'

'What do you want?' Josie's immediate instinct was to retreat, prevaricate, not to commit.

'I need to write a letter to Wayne; they won't let me ring him, see.'

'So?' Josie was still cautious.

Joyce took a deep breath. 'I can't really write, or read, yer see. Yer know they're trying to teach me literacy in Education but it's so complicated; I'm not getting on at all. Will you 'elp me write something to him?'

'Okay. After supper do?' That shouldn't be too onerous, she thought.

'Yeah, thanks.'

Josie had her hand on the door; she turned back to the waif-like girl on the bed in her grubby jersey and stained tracksuit trousers. She remembered the self-harm slashes on the thin arms. She wasn't sure what she was going to say and the words came out almost as if someone else had made the decision to speak.

'D'you want me to help teach you to read and write, then?'

'You'd do that, then?' Joyce looked surprised. 'For me?'

'If you want me to.'

'Oh yeah, please.' The delight on Joyce's thin little face was palpable.

Chapter 21

ONCE AGAIN JOSIE WAS SITTING in Sadie Harrison's cramped little office. Sadie had pushed her glasses on top of her head and in her hand was a letter that she had just finished reading out to Josie.

'So, Jo, what do you make of that, then?'

Josie frowned and bit her lip. 'She seems very...' she paused, trying to find the right word '...considerate.'

Sadie put the letter on her desk and leant forward. 'So, what do you think you should do now?'

The letter was from Mrs Brodinski, Tomas's mother. It had been written by Tomas's sister, Sophia, who had translated for her mother. Mrs Brodinski had said how desperately she missed her son; how deeply upset she had been at the news of his accident and death. She was a widow and she had gone on to say that she also missed his financial support as he had been sending money home from England earned from his work as an electrician. The money was in part being used to help Sophia through college in Warsaw. Life was a lot more difficult for both of them without his help. She said that she understood it was an accident and that the perpetrator – she didn't mention Josie by name – must also have been upset and, she hoped, repentant. Yes, she had no objection to receiving a letter from the perpetrator and hoped that in writing that person might find a little comfort. She said she was sorry that a prison sentence had been imposed as she didn't think it would help anyone.

A feeling of dread settled on Josie's stomach. How could I write anything meaningful or appropriate to this compassionate woman? Anything I wrote would sound trite and pathetic. Her son lost his life because I was unable to deal with a stupid, opportunistic, arrogant creep of a man. How sad is that? These and other thoughts raced round Josie's head. She was aware that Mrs Harrison was still waiting for a reply.

'I should write back to her.' Her voice was flat and she looked at the letter on the desk and not at Sadie.

'Yes, you should. It won't be easy, will it? Now, I'm taking some leave over Christmas so I shan't see you till mid-January. I want you to have a draft letter on my desk when we next meet. We can agree it then and get it sent off.'

Josie nodded miserably.

After Josie had left Sadie sat with her chin cupped in her hand. That was interesting, she thought. It was clear that Josie was upset by the conciliatory tone of the letter, but Sadie was pretty sure there would be a draft reply waiting when she was back in the office. There had been no denials, prevarication or justification from Josie over writing the letter, or for not doing so either. Sadie looked through the case notes: 'At no time during our interviews has Miss Anderson given any indication as to why she was driving so badly on the night of the accident. She has refused to provide excuses or reasons.'

'Well, we'll see' Sadie said aloud. 'Writing the letter may just unlock something.' She put the folder marked J Anderson AT119360A back into her 'pending' tray and resettled her glasses on her nose.

Chapter 22

IT WAS THE EVENING of the Carol Service. The choir, some two dozen women, including Amy, Sharon and Josie, had rehearsed once a week with the chaplain; the piano was played by Lesley, a lifer who, Josie learned in horror, had poisoned her husband many years ago, had been the centre of a high-profile court case and had been a music teacher in her previous existence. She had reluctantly agreed some years ago to play for the annual Carol Service as well as for services in the chapel.

Josie looked into her little mirror as she scraped her hair back and prepared to put a scrunchy round her ponytail. She stopped and frowned at herself, letting her hair fall to her shoulders again. Perhaps she should leave it loose for once. It was clean and shiny, she had washed it the previous evening, and it felt a bit more festive and party-like swinging round her face. She turned her head from side to side, trying to see a true reflection in the inadequate glass. Yes, loose it should be. She didn't have anything pretty to wear, just a clean white shirt and her corduroy trousers. It didn't matter; she expected to be sitting in the back row of the choir anyway and no one would look at her except when she and Amy were singing the first verse of 'Once in Royal David's City.' She was dreading it, but singing with Amy meant they could rely on each other. There was strength in numbers, she decided, even if there were only the two of them.

She was jolted out of her thoughts by a tannoy announcement calling everyone for the Carol Service. A few moments later the officers arrived in Beech House to escort the women to the visits centre where the service would be held.

There were rows and rows of chairs laid out in a semicircle facing a small rostrum that had enough chairs on it for the choir and for the chaplain and her team. The piano had been wheeled into position on one side and there was a wooden lectern at the front of the rostrum. Josie and Sharon joined the other members of the choir. Josie edged round the chairs to her designated seat in the back row and sat down to wait. Amy hadn't arrived yet, which was odd as other women from her house were already there. The Governor and his guests came in through the main door and everyone quietened down and moved to their places. Still there was no Amy. The chaplain came over to the rostrum and rearranged her service sheets; she looked at her watch and then turned to check the choir behind her. Josie tried to get her attention by pointing to Amy's empty seat, but she didn't see. Lesley, the pianist, sat down and adjusted her piano stool and as she looked up Josie managed to catch her eye and desperately mouthed 'Amy' at her. Lesley looked initially perplexed but then nodded in understanding and got up and whispered to the chaplain.

Josie was tense with apprehension. She watched as the chaplain consulted one of the prison officers who shook his head ominously. The chaplain came over to Josie.

'I'm afraid Amy's not well, a stomach upset,' she whispered, 'she won't be here. You'll have to sing on your own. You'll be fine.' She put her hand on Josie's arm in encouragement.

'No. I can't.' Josie was aghast.

'Jo, you can and you will; you can't let the others down. You'll be fine. Take a deep breath now and relax. You can do it. We have to start, it's six-thirty and I can see the Governor getting restive.' She patted Josie's arm again, turned back to the rostrum and began to welcome everyone.

Josie looked across at Lesley in desperation as if willing her not to play; Lesley made an encouraging smile across the piano then immediately began the opening bars of 'Once in Royal David's City'. Josie felt her left hand being gripped; it was Sharon on her other side who whispered 'Go on kiddo, we're with you.' Josie took a deep breath.

Chapter 23

THE PRISON HAD BEEN quiet for an hour or more and Josie lay in her little bed listening to the silence. Despite her new blue flame-retardant curtains hanging stiffly over the small window she could still see the orange glow of the security light outside Beech House. It had become as familiar as the stained ceiling and the battered door, the latter being reminders of past occupants whom Josie could only guess at and whose crimes remained lingering in the history of Edgehill. Sometimes Josie wondered what had happened to these women. She hoped they were all right on the outside, with family and friends who cared about them.

For the umpteenth time that night she thought back over the Carol Service. She relived the moment she realised that she was going to have to sing solo, remembering the feeling of absolute panic that had gripped her. Her hands clutched her duvet as the opening bars of the carol sounded again in her ears. Without Sharon's encouraging grasp throughout that first verse she knew she couldn't have done it. Yet she had done it and her singing, whilst not being very special, was good enough, had been in tune and was seemingly audible throughout the visits centre. She knew this because so many people came up to her after the service and said nice things. Even the Governor patted her on the back and told her he was proud of her.

'Well done, Josephine,' he had said. 'You sang well and you showed courage.' He had smiled warmly and introduced her to the local mayor who shook her hand and added his congratulations.

The rest of the service had passed in a dream; Josie had stood up and sat down as required and sung the choir-only pieces as directed but encompassing her throughout was the unfamiliar feeling of having achieved something memorable. Something she had never done before, indeed never been asked to do before, and the memory was sweet. She wished she could tell her Dad about it, he would have been proud.

'Mind now,' he would have said, 'No boasting. You're better than no one and no one is better than you.' Then he would have smiled and said 'Good on you, Josie, that's my girl.'

Josie sighed and turned over in bed. Today could be ticked off on her calendar and tomorrow would be another day closer to her release. Then she remembered Amy and hoped she was all right; it would be good to relive it all again with her if she was better in the morning. Another, more unwelcome thought struck her: she knew she really must make a proper start tomorrow on writing the dreaded letter to Mrs Brodinski.

Chapter 24

CHRISTMAS WAS A NOTORIOUSLY difficult time for the inmates of Edgehill: some women had been permitted home leave for a few days, especially if they were close to the end of their sentences. Others had been refused leave; they congregated in small, disillusioned groups outside the dining room or at meals, their mood mutinous, angry and resentful at the perceived injustice. The prison staff, stretched thinly over the festive season when many of their colleagues had been granted leave, were apt to pick on the women for small offences that normally they would either have ignored or dealt with leniently. The feeling of tension was palpable throughout the prison and the segregation unit was full.

Christmas Eve came. Several times the alarm bells were activated in different parts of the campus, warning exhausted officers that the atmosphere was becoming increasingly febrile.

Josie had become expert at avoiding difficult confrontations with women she either disliked or distrusted, of whom there were many. She avoided public places as much as possible and didn't often join others in the association room unless she knew Sharon or Michelle were there as they acted as unofficial referees and were generally respected. But both of them had been granted home leave so there was no one to hide behind this particular evening. Sometimes she went to the library but it was now shut for the Christmas period so she had little option but to stay in her own room, looking at the few Christmas cards she had received and thinking about her last Christmas at home just before her father had died. It had been a lovely day, just the two of them. Homesickness now choked her as she remembered cooking the turkey crown – a whole turkey would have been too much, they had decided – and then having a pleasant walk round the local lanes before watching the Queen and a Downton Christmas Special on television. They had a small glass of sweet sherry to celebrate. Her Dad had put up a tree in the sitting room, a real one, none of that artificial trash, as he called it. She had decorated it with all the usual bits and pieces from the box he had fetched down from the attic, including the special star and the twinkly lights. On the end of the mantelpiece she had arranged the wooden nativity scene, given to her mother by an old aunt who had worked in Nigeria. Joseph, Mary and the Baby were black, but it didn't seem to matter that the Shepherds and Angel Gabriel were white; the group just fitted in neatly beside the mahogany chiming clock. It had seemed such a happy day.

Tears rolled silently down her cheeks as she lay on her bed listening to the noises in the passage outside her room. Today and last year could hardly be more different and it wasn't even Christmas until tomorrow; could things get worse? Self-pity welled up and she couldn't find the energy to dispel it. She turned on her tummy and buried her face in her pillow.

'Jo, Jo, come on!' Joyce was banging on her door in excitement. 'They're judging best-decorated house and we're in the last three.'

Josie got up reluctantly, wiped her eyes with her hand and opened the door. The other residents of Beech House were lining the passage or looking out of their doors as the governor and two senior officers, notebooks in hand, were walking slowly down the corridor looking at the home-made decorations festooning the walls. They inspected the association room and the entrance lobby and very seriously made notes as they went.

'I'll be announcing the winner at supper time,' the Governor said as they went out.

'Oh, I do hope it's us,' Joyce said. 'First prize is a big tin of Quality Street, yer know. I just love the ones in the shiny purple wrapping.'

'We're not likely to win and the sweets won't go far between twenty of us if we do,' Josie said and then saw Joyce's face fall. 'Though I suppose we've got as good a chance of winning as any other house.'

Chapter 25

RAIN FELL FROM A LEADEN SKY. Everywhere was grey: paths, roofs, trees; the prison inmates, with their heads down and hoods up seemed drab and colourless as they scurried from building to building trying to escape the wet. Christmas, with its bright lights and cheer, real or imagined, was over. The decorations were still hanging forlornly in the houses and the Christmas trees in the dining room and visits centre still stood, stark and lonely, their decorations packed away for another year.

There had been several incidents of hooch being brewed by prisoners in Beech House – using fruit or bread stolen from the kitchens. Officers had to deal with rowdy women and aggressive behaviour. Sanctions had been imposed, inevitably adding to the feelings of resentment. Josie tried to avoid being drawn into the conflict.

To pass the time before work restarted she persuaded Joyce to have a reading session, but it hadn't been fruitful. Joyce's concentration at the best of times was fitful, but she seemed unable to make sense of even the most fundamental sentences and Josie's patience was sorely tested. She doubted her own abilities as a teacher but also recognised that Joyce's academic aptitude was very limited. In the end she had closed the reading book and handed it silently to Joyce, who looked hurt, and then returned to her own room to read a novel instead. Still the unwritten letter to Mrs Brodinski hung over her.

Mr P had said he might come in to catch up on some long-overdue paperwork at the end of December and had told her that if she wanted to work on her own in the polytunnels then that was fine by him. He would unlock the gate for her and she could carry on with potting on some of the late summer cuttings that were getting overcrowded. She decided to accept his offer and as she reached the polytunnel she could see him through the window of his office sitting at his desk. She waved at him and he returned her greeting with a smile and a thumbs-up.

The polytunnel was warm and dry and the familiar smell of geranium leaves and compost greeted her as she slid the door open. After the few days of feverish Christmas excitement followed by the general feeling of unrest, the polytunnel seemed an oasis of calm; Josie unconsciously let out a sigh of relief. She shut the door behind her, then dragged the old metal stool across to the bench and filled the first of the waiting flowerpots with new compost. To be out of her room and alone, just for an hour or two, was wonderful.

She arranged the completed pots in a square eight deep. It was very satisfying filling row after row of pots and lining them up like soldiers until the square was finished. That made sixty-four new plants. There were still three more containers to do, each with about a dozen cuttings, so in total, she reckoned, there would be about a hundred geranium plants ready to be transplanted into the beds around the prison by the end of May. For a brief moment she felt saddened that she wouldn't be here to do the work. It would have been good to see the cheerful red, white and pink flowers brightening up the campus for the summer. As she turned to get more compost she remembered the letter. Reluctantly she tried to concentrate on what she would write to Mrs Brodinski. She would apologise, of course, but it would be inadequate; should she give reasons or make excuses for the accident? No, she decided; that would be a pitiful thing to do. In her head, as she methodically and automatically lined up more cuttings on the bench, she composed a first draft of the letter. Time and again she rephrased the sentences, hoping that when she returned to her room after lunch she would remember what she had intended to say and wouldn't have to start all over again when she came to write it out. She was so engrossed in her thoughts that she didn't hear Mr P entering the polytunnel until she realised he was standing beside her.

'You're doing a good job, Jo.' He picked up a pot and tested the firmness of the compost with his forefinger. 'They'll need a drink when you've finished, but not much or they'll get botrytis if we're not careful. Keep the water off the leaves.'

She nodded as she emptied the last pot of cuttings onto the bench to see how many had rooted.

'I must go in a moment but I thought I'd let you know it looks as if funding is going to be provided for a second member of staff to help me and so we might be able to restart the City and Guilds horticultural diploma course. Do you remember we talked about it in our last Gardens' meeting?'

Again she nodded and put down her pot, looking up at him with interest as he went on.

'Some of you expressed an interest in working for a qualification; I think you were one of them?'

'I'd like to, but it depends how long it would take.'

'When's your release date?'

'Early May, I hope.'

'Could be tight. You might have to put in extra hours.' Sensing her unspoken uncertainty he went on 'Do you have a job waiting for you when you go out, then?'

'I don't know; probably not.' She bit her lip, unwilling to discuss it.

'Where's home?'

She told him and then turned to pick up the watering can.

'Did you know there are two rather good plant nurseries near there?'

She shook her head as she carefully dribbled water onto the cuttings, making sure they weren't too wet.

'You know what I think?'

'No.'

'You have a natural ability with plants, and your work has been exemplary. If you wanted a career in horticulture you could do very well.' He put his head on one side and looked at her enquiringly.

'Thank you.' This was a new thought and it was nice being praised. 'When do you need to know if I want to do the course?' She put the watering can back down on the floor.

'I should have confirmation next week of the funding. When we start again on Monday we can talk about it. What do you think?'

'Yes, but where can I find out what it entails and where it might lead – job-wise, that is?'

You probably can't as you don't have internet access. I'll get as much info as I can before Monday and we'll take it from there. Okay?'

She nodded.

'Now, finish off or you'll be late for roll call and I must lock up.' He waited a few moments whilst she tidied up the bench and put on her anorak, then he ushered her out into the chilly January day.

'See you Monday,' he called as he hurried away towards the gatehouse.

Josie watched him stride down the path. The thought of a job in horticulture was a new one and she looked forward to thinking it through when she was back in her room after lunch. It was good to have something positive to consider. Now she needed to get a move on to avoid being marked as absent from the lunchtime roll call.

To reach the dining room she had to pass two of the residential houses that were set at right angles to the path; she was deep in thought about the gardening course, unaware of anything or anyone around her when she heard a scream from the first house, Rowan, she thought the house was called. She jerked her head round to see what was going on. It wasn't unusual to hear disturbances of one sort or another in the houses and her normal reaction was to ignore whatever it was and get out of the way, but before she had time to do either, two women, whom she didn't know, catapulted out of Rowan, one chasing the other. She was directly in their way. The first woman cannoned into Josie almost knocking her down, then, recovering her own balance, the woman fled towards the second house. The pursuer had a broken bottle in her hand. Realising she had lost her intended prey she lunged at Josie and grabbed her round the neck brandishing the bottle in her face.

'Yer fuckin' comin' with me,' she screamed and pulled Josie back across the path towards a small building used by enhanced prisoners. She kicked the door open, manhandled Josie inside and shoved her into a small store room.

'Sit down. Don't move or yer'll fuckin' get this in yer face.'

Josie did as she was told. The woman was larger than her and muscular. The bottle had a hideously jagged edge. Then she heard the alarms going off.

Still brandishing the bottle the woman used her other hand to barricade the doorway with two chairs and a piece of shelving. She and Josie were on the inside.

It seemed to take forever for officers to arrive but was probably only a minute or two. Backed against the wall in the small room, her legs uncomfortably bent under her and with the woman's right foot wedged into her chest whilst the bottle remained ominously close to her face, Josie tried to keep calm. All her instincts were to scream as loudly as she could. The woman must have guessed this.

'Not a fuckin' word outa yer or yer get this down yer fuckin' throat.' She shoved her foot harder into Josie's chest. The bottle was inches from Josie's eyes.

The outside door of the building crashed open and four officers charged into the tiny corridor.

'Keep back or she fuckin' gets it,' screamed the woman.

Assessing the situation the officers immediately backed off and Josie could hear their radios crackling with urgent messages to the communications room.

It wasn't long before a female officer appeared in the doorway on her own.

'Not another friggin' step.' The woman's voice was hoarse with menace and she didn't remove her foot from Josie's chest or the bottle from her face.

'It's okay, Noreen, I won't come any closer but I need to know what all this is about. Perhaps we can have a little chat?' The tone of voice was gentle and conciliatory. 'Perhaps you can let Jo leave while we talk?'

'Not bloody likely. She gets it if yer don't do as I say.'

'Well, how about you pull up one of those chairs and sit down and I'll sit out here and then we can get to the bottom of this?'

'Nah. I'll tell yer what I want and I'll use this' – she waved the bottle – 'on her,' gesturing at Josie, 'if I don't bloody get it.'

There was no doubting her intentions. Paralysed with fear as she was, Josie realised that the situation would be protracted. She might remain a hostage for hours. Her right leg, still bent under her, had cramp, there was a table leg jammed into her left shoulder and her head was forced forward by a shelf fixed to the wall behind her. Noreen's right foot, shod in a heavy work boot, didn't shift from her chest.

Josie had known fright before: Mike's assault had been frightening; the journey in the van had been terrifying; she had been scared witless by the woman pushing her over in the dining room and by Joyce's attempted suicide, but this was worse. Much worse, and she was completely powerless. Her life depended on the quiet talking of the woman officer whom she couldn't even see from her position on the floor.

Noreen, inarticulate and incoherent with anger and pent-up emotion, attempted to outline her demands to the officer. Her home leave had been refused over Christmas, she wanted to be transferred to a prison closer to Manchester and she wanted access to her children, who had been taken into care. Again and again she reiterated her demands. After an hour had passed the officer was relieved by another negotiator, also a woman. The tactics changed but still the officer insisted that no demands would be considered until Josie, the hostage, had been released. Only then would the prison authorities listen seriously to Noreen's grievances.

The situation seemed to Josie to have reached an irreconcilable impasse. Where was the Governor? What was he doing? What was happening in the incident room? She knew her own safety was priority and that gave her some comfort even though she remained only too aware of the proximity of the bottle and the fickleness of Noreen's emotions. A wrong move by the negotiator could prove fatal.

Josie became fixated on the broken bottle. Depending on Noreen's mood it regularly hovered between six inches and a foot from her face, its jagged edges menacingly close to her eyes. Occasionally the daylight from the passage glinted on the glass, causing a fleeting reflection to shine malevolently across Noreen's embittered face. Several times Josie tried to put her arms up to protect her own face but each time it prompted further aggression from Noreen. She stayed as still as she could and silently followed the movements of the deadly weapon.

Two hours passed. Eventually Noreen had been persuaded to take her foot off Josie's chest and had accepted a drink of water and a sandwich. She had reluctantly passed a drink to Josie too. Briefly Josie allowed herself to believe that Noreen was capitulating; but then, completely illogically, she resumed her threatening stance with the bottle. She planted her foot back on Josie's chest, forcing her to the floor once again. Another negotiator took over.

It began to get dark. Noreen refused to switch the store room light on. The electric light from the passage shone in at an angle, partially illuminating the centre of the room but leaving Josie in semi-darkness. No one had spoken to her for a long time and she, too, had remained silent, a passive figure in the drama, but nonetheless a central one.

Then, suddenly, it was all over. Josie, acutely conscious of every twist and turn of the negotiations, was taken by surprise at the rapidity and efficiency of the rescue when it came. With lightning speed six officers in full protective gear, wearing helmets, and carrying batons and shields had arrived in the passage beside the negotiator. Two of them rushed the barricade, floored Noreen and removed the bottle. The lack of space in the little store room meant that the other four officers had to wait until their colleagues had disarmed Noreen before they were able to assist in the restraint and with helping Josie to her feet. What had prompted their intervention at that point Josie had no idea. Why had the negotiations been abandoned? Noreen hadn't seemed to relax her guard, nor had Josie heard the men assembling outside the building prior to their entry. Something must have triggered their action, or maybe the incident room had given the order because of a new risk that Josie knew nothing about. It didn't matter; she was free. Noreen was marched off under restraint by the six officers to the segregation unit. Josie, shaking uncontrollably from head to foot, was wrapped in a blanket and checked over by the medical team. Later she was given a meal and allowed back to her room accompanied by an officer who stayed with her until the counselling team took over.

She was exhausted, but she was free.

Chapter 26

WHAT THE HELL did yer do that for, yer fuckin' cunt?'
Josie turned round. She was returning a book to
the library a few days later. Behind her were three women
whom she only knew by sight as friends of Noreen.

'Soddin' bitch, why did yer split on Noreen?'

They were all looking at her.

'I didn't. I don't know what you mean.'

The women surrounded her.

'She doesn't know what we mean,' one of them jeered,
imitating her voice.

'Yer shite, yer know,' the second one said, pushing her
face close to Josie's.

They jostled Josie, pushing her off the path and onto
the flower bed. Her book fell to the ground.

'Leave me alone; I don't know what you're talking about.'
She tried to get past them and back onto the path.

One of the women kicked the book under a bush.
Another shoved her hard from behind and she fell to her
knees.

'Yer got 'er shipped out, yer slimy toad. Yer deserve what's
comin' to yer.'

Before Josie could do anything two officers appeared.
The aggressors quickly backed off but not before their names
and numbers were taken. The male officer escorted them
away.

'You all right, Jo?' the woman officer asked, helping her
to her feet.

'I think so.' Josie brushed leaves and twigs off her trousers and bent down to retrieve the book. She felt shaken and frightened. 'But I don't understand why they thought I had anything to do with Noreen before she attacked me. I didn't even know her.'

'Prison gossip probably. They were part of her little gang and needed someone to blame when she was moved out. They'll get their come-uppance when we've filed a report. Just so long as you're not hurt?'

Josie shook her head. She didn't want to admit to herself or the officer how intimidated she had felt. Since the hostage incident she had found herself the centre of attention on various occasions. She hadn't liked it and wanted life to get back to normal, insofar as prison life was normal.

Chapter 27

COLD WEATHER SET IN during January. The prisoners woke one morning to find a thick covering of snow across the campus. Most of the women were from big cities and actively disliked snow. There was a lot of grumbling and many attempts made to avoid going outside for work or education and even meals.

Josie had also thought of snow as a nuisance. It was all right when it had just fallen but she hated having her best leather boots ruined with unsightly water marks; she disliked the grey sludge that sprayed up on her car windscreen; she loathed having to leave the warmth of her house to put the bins out or empty the kitchen waste. Now, despite the moans from the other girls, she looked at it with new eyes. The drabness of the prison buildings was temporarily camouflaged; the perimeter wire had several inches of snow precariously perched on top, creating a filigree effect that was magical as the sun shone through it. Its purpose seemed diminished. The shrubs and trees lost their twiggy individuality and settled snugly and contentedly beneath their pristine blankets like giant, sleeping dinosaurs. Briefly the low-lying January sun glinted on the snowy rooftops creating thousands of tiny sparkles. The sparrows swooped down from their chilly perches, chattering noisily with delight when the women shared their breakfast bread with them. For a few precious hours the grim distinguishing marks of the prison were obliterated under the thick, white duvet.

Soon, however, the works department was out with tractors and spades clearing the paths and liberally sprinkling grit along the main thoroughfares. By the end of the morning clouds, heavy with rain, rolled across the horizon from the north, enveloping the transient winter sunshine. The drab, utilitarian landscape re-emerged once more, reflecting the greyness of the sky. The banks of snow lining the sides of the paths were thawing into gravelly heaps.

Later that morning Mr P called his gardening girls to a meeting in his office. They, too, had helped with the snow clearing and now, pleased to be back indoors, they stood close to his fan heater, blowing their hands and stamping their feet to keep warm while he outlined the implementation of the horticultural diploma for which funding had now been found, and explained that a new tutor was about to join them. There was much discussion. Josie and five others had already told him that they would like to work for the diploma, so he handed out all the information with a schedule and course books.

'We can't do any more outdoor work today,' he said. 'So go away and read all the paperwork and come back tomorrow. We'll have another chat about it first thing. Then I want some of you to get on with pruning the apple trees at the back of the allotment area and the rest of you to continue tidying the polytunnels. Off you go.'

They trudged back along the thawing paths to their houses, pleased to have the rest of the day indoors.

Josie settled down on her bed to read about the course work she would have to do. It seemed fairly straightforward and she had already covered quite a few of the modules, such as health and safety and tool maintenance, which was helpful. Mr P had also given her details of two plant nurseries that weren't too far from Northwood and had kindly printed out information from their websites for her.

She tried to think about a post-prison life. What would it be like? Could she still live in Northwood? Would the people she knew there want to speak to her after what she had done? Would anyone offer a job to an ex-offender? Was she any good at anything anyway? Waves of self-doubt swept over her. All the things that had gone wrong in the last six months must mean she was a rubbish sort of person, didn't they?

Everything suddenly seemed overwhelmingly difficult.

Chapter 28

Mrs Harrison looked at the young woman sitting opposite her. When they had last met a month ago she had been impressed that Josie had agreed to write the letter to Mrs Brodinski without prevarication. It was true she hadn't been enthusiastic but Mrs Harrison had noted a spark of determination. Josie had shown grit. There had even been a hint of initiative. Sadie guessed that most of her other clients would have refused to co-operate at all with such a difficult task.

Josie had indeed written the required letter and from a cursory glance at it Sadie thought it looked more than adequate. But what bothered her as she looked at Josie was her current demeanour. Something must have gone badly wrong since their last meeting. Josie sat with her head down, her hands twisting in her lap, her hair looked unwashed and her clothes were not very clean. Where was her self-respect? This looked more like the girl she had met in her first week in the prison: low self-esteem, lacking self-confidence and permeating resignation. Where was the motivation she had begun to show at their last meeting before Christmas? If Sadie didn't know better from having seen negative drug-testing results she might well have thought Josie had fallen in with the substance misuse crowd.

Sadie had made it her business to find out all the details of the hostage incident when she had read about it in the prison's weekly bulletin, though Josie wasn't named. When she had learned that it was Josie, she had immediately been concerned for the repercussions it might have on her. Looking at the unhappy woman sitting in front of her she was pretty sure she understood the cause of her apparent misery and dejection. Traumatic events often triggered unexpected reactions. But what was to be done about it? Firstly they needed to discuss the letter and that could, she thought, be a positive process to start unravelling the apparent problem.

Sadie rearranged her glasses on her nose and picked up Josie's letter to Mrs Brodinski.

'Wait for a moment, Jo, while I read this properly,' she said.

Josie lifted her head and listlessly gazed out of the small window. She could just see the path that led to the Offender Managers' Unit, where she now sat. Flanking the path like prison guards were three tall shrub roses, skeletal apart from a couple of tattered yellowing leaves grimly hanging on to the stems. She and Amy had been asked to prune the roses just before Christmas: not too much, Mr P had said, just enough to stop wind rock. She noticed that they had missed a couple of stems that now stuck out sideways from the main plant; probably the snow had weighted them down. I ought to cut them off tomorrow or they will break and maybe tear the stem, she thought. Then the effort of doing so felt too much and she thought that perhaps she couldn't be bothered. No one would notice if she didn't do it. She refocused as Sadie Harrison was speaking to her again; wearily Josie tried to concentrate on what she was saying.

'So, I think you have done very well here, Jo. This is pretty much what I wanted. I suggest we just amend a couple of details, if you agree, and then I'll send it off. I am impressed with the way you have taken responsibility for what happened and yet not made any fatuous excuses or proffered unlikely reasons for your behaviour. It is a dignified and yet contrite letter. Well done, I think Mrs Brodinski will be pleased.'

Josie barely reacted to the praise.

'Now,' Sadie continued, having noted the apathy. 'I expect you are fed up to the back teeth with people asking you about the hostage incident?'

Josie nodded.

'I thought so. But let us just spend a few moments talking about the consequences of the incident rather than the incident itself – I daresay the counsellors did that too?'

Again Josie nodded and looked at her lap.

'I'm sure they did but I think it might also be helpful to look at it again.'

Josie looked up, puzzled.

Sadie leaned back in her chair.

'What did you feel when the incident was over?'

'Relief, I suppose,'

'How did the other inmates react to you afterwards?'

'Most of the women in Beech House were supportive, I suppose, and kind.'

'What about other prisoners; friends of Noreen's for instance?'

Josie paused for a moment. Her voice dropped. 'They seemed to think I was to blame.' She slumped further into her chair.

'Why do you say that?'

'They said it was my fault that Noreen was so angry and then that she was shipped out. They said I had split on her. But I didn't even know her.'

'What do you think about that?' Sadie kept her tone of voice conversational.

'At first I didn't understand. I didn't see how they could say those things. Then I wondered if they were right. Maybe I had done something to upset Noreen, even though I didn't know what, so maybe I deserved to be attacked.'

'Why do you think that?'

Josie looked directly at Sadie. She sat up in her chair and gripped the edge of the table in front of her. There were tears in her eyes; her voice rose:

'I seem to make such rubbish decisions all the time. Nothing I do seems to work. It's all my fault; having the accident; being in here; upsetting Noreen; being pushed over; everything; even being tripped up in the dining hall, maybe Joyce's suicide attempt. I deserve to be in here, no doubt of that, and I don't deserve another chance. I am so, so stupid. I don't know why.' She slumped back in her chair again as tears rolled down her cheeks.

'Let's unpick a bit of that, shall we?' Sadie said calmly, passing a tissue from the box on her desk. 'Go back to the beginning. What was the 'rubbish decision', as you call it, which caused the accident?'

'Letting what Mike did upset me.' In her misery Josie had forgotten that she had never mentioned Mike to anyone other than Di.

It all poured out. She recounted tearfully the week of *The Mikado* and what had happened; she told Sadie about Mike's unexpected and unwanted advances and her own inability to deal with him. Then she explained how the accident had happened because of her blind panic. How the police had mercilessly interrogated her and then how

David Owens' efforts to get her to provide mitigation had failed because she had felt unable to make excuses or explain. Because she thought she was to blame.

Sadie Harrison had years of experience with prisoners and before that with abused children; she knew intuitively where to press and when to hold back and let the revelations come. She knew better than to contradict a client who professed to being inadequate or 'rubbish' as Josie was doing. The floodgates had opened; best let the water pour out and see where it flowed.

An hour later Josie was still sitting opposite Sadie Harrison. Her tears had stopped though she continued to clutch a soggy tissue and the bin beside the desk contained many more. She felt worn out but strangely relieved.

Sadie, on the other hand, was surprised at the revelations that poured out. She had deliberately led Jo back through her life to try and ascertain why she lacked the confidence and ability to deal with a predator like Mike. Almost any other girl from her background and with her education would have had no problem putting him in his place and would not have panicked as Jo so obviously had and with such disastrous results. It was also important to find out why Jo had refused to implicate Mike in the subsequent accident as he certainly deserved it and it would probably have made such a fundamental difference to the imposition of her ultimate sentence. What was Jo hiding?

The answer to both these questions eventually materialised. It wasn't what Sadie was expecting, even though, in her extensive experience, answers were apt to lie in childhood events. She knew better, however, than to express her surprise.

Chapter 29

LATE EVENING NOISE in Beech House filtered under Josie's door as she lay in bed waiting for sleep. Doors of individual rooms slammed shut; calls of 'goodnight', often followed by a 'shut up' from a third party, could be heard, and the muffled noise of televisions seeped into the communal passage. No arguments or fights tonight, Josie noticed with relief.

She turned onto her back and stared up into the darkness. Why did I tell her? I was never going to tell anyone. We'd done nothing wrong; we hadn't hurt anyone; it was 'our little secret', he'd said. We hadn't even hurt Mum, he'd said. Mum hadn't wanted it anyway. What she didn't know wouldn't hurt her, he'd said.

She remembered the tip-toeing steps up the stairs and the gentle tap at her door. Later, after Mum had died, the tip-toeing stopped but there was still a tap. He was always so considerate and gentle. She did miss him dreadfully after he died.

What had she done by telling Mrs Harrison? Dread seized her and she screwed the top of the duvet into a sausage and twisted it tightly in her agony. What would happen now? Would other people need to know too? Would she have to talk about it? It wasn't the same as Joyce and all those so-called uncles. Now that really had been abuse. Hers had been a kind and loving relationship, hadn't it? It absolutely wasn't anyone else's business; she categorically wouldn't talk about it again. They couldn't make her. But Mrs Harrison was telling her she must attend therapy sessions. 'I can't do it,' she screamed inwardly, 'they can't make me.'

Stricken with guilt and filled with fear and worry, the sense of relief she had experienced earlier long dissipated, Josie restlessly tossed and turned until a grey January dawn woke the resident blackbirds outside her window and sleep became impossible.

Chapter 30

AFTER A WEEK OF non-co-operation with the prison rehabilitation team Josie had been sitting in her room after returning from her gardening duties. There was a knock on the door. Since her traumatic meeting with Mrs Harrison she had taken to locking herself in her room and refusing to communicate with the other women. She ignored the knock and hoped whoever was there would go away.

'Jo, I know yer there, I saw yer come in. Unlock the door.' It was Sharon.

Reluctantly Josie got up from her bed and turned the key. She didn't bother to open the door but returned to her bed and sat down again facing away. Sharon entered and crossed to the end of the bed where she stood in silence for a moment waiting for Josie to acknowledge her.

'Yer got to help yerself, Jo. Yer know that,' she stated bluntly when Josie continued to stare silently at the wall.

There was no reply.

'Yer letting yerself down and yer letting all yer friends down, too, don't yer see?'

Josie shook her head.

'So what about Joyce? She's really upset cos she thinks she's done somethin' to make yer cross with 'er. Yer've not done any readin' with 'er for ages or helped 'er with her canteen sheet and she thinks it's 'er fault. What you gonna do about that, then?'

Josie mumbled something unintelligible.

'C'mon, Jo.' Sharon sat on the bed beside Josie. 'Yer not the only one in here who's been messed about by their old man. But yer've got to deal with it kiddo. Tisn't the end of the world.'

Josie turned round angrily.

'Who told you?'

'I'm a peer mentor. It's my job to be told stuff. S'all right, the others don't know.' Sharon looked with concern at Josie. Her careworn face was creased with anxiety. Sensing a slight relaxing by the younger woman Sharon put an arm round her.

'C'mon, Jo,' she said again. 'Let's talk it through.'

Reluctantly Josie listened to Sharon. Gradually she allowed the other woman to persuade her to consider that she might need the help that was on offer. By the time the call for supper came an hour later she had agreed to go to one of the one-to-one sessions that had been arranged, just to see what it was about. She wasn't prepared to commit to any more as yet.

'Yer've got to get this sorted in yer head before yer go out, yer know,' Sharon said.

Josie gave her a sideways glance. As far as she was concerned there was nothing to be sorted but if going to one session got Sharon and Mrs Harrison off her back maybe it would be worth complying.

'We'd better get to supper.' Sharon got up. 'Let's see if Joyce is in 'er room and yer can arrange to read with 'er after?' She patted Josie's arm encouragingly.

Chapter 31

JANUARY MERGED SEAMLESSLY into February. Josie continued to cross the days off on her calendar. It was the cheapest calendar available in the prison's catalogue, bought using the £10-a-week earnings from her garden work. The photographs of cute animals in picturesque gardens were a cruel reminder of other people's domestic bliss. She thought longingly of Northwood, not that it was particularly photogenic; too many unedifying council houses built in slap-dash rows, interspersed with equally unedifying fifties semis. There was a nice Norman church and a few, a very few, black and white houses set in pretty gardens and owned by retired professional people, but mostly it was a rather bog-standard ribbon development. But it was home. And she wanted to be back there.

She was now half-way through her sentence. Every day crossed off on the calendar meant she was one step closer to release. But the pictures of cosy kittens in wicker baskets, the adorable puppies with limpid brown eyes and the shaggy ponies frolicking in immaculate fields near the chocolate-box houses were not reality. Reality, she knew, was finishing her sentence, getting a job, returning to Northwood and dealing with what that might entail.

Reality, according to Sadie Harrison, was putting the past behind her and understanding and coming to terms with the fact that she, Josie, was as much a victim as Mrs Brodinski and Tomas. Josie didn't see it like that and refused to co-operate in the therapy sessions. She became angry;

it was no one's business but her own; how dare the prison interfere; she didn't need their help. She was not like the other women. It was pointed out to her that 50 per cent of the women in Edgehill had been abused. Despite what Sharon and Sadie Harrison had said she refused to accept that she was one of them. She was told she had suffered trauma not just because of her father but also because of being taken hostage by Noreen. She was told these traumatic events had influenced her reasoning and affected her relationships with other people. She wouldn't listen.

Chapter 32

GRADUALLY AND INEXORABLY as the weeks rolled by the therapy sessions did what they were intended to do. Josie, metaphorically kicking and screaming, was persuaded to face the incontrovertible truth of what her father had done to her. There had been highs and lows during her prison sentence before this but now she felt as if she was teetering on the edge of the deepest crevasse of all and beyond it was a seemingly impassable mountain. Everything she had known before prison was a lie, an enormous untruth; her whole life was now based on falsehoods. She wasn't who she thought she was. She attempted to balance precariously on the treacherous edge of the crevasse; one false step and she would slip and be consumed in self-pity and failure in the beckoning abyss, but to make progress over it and start on the long climb upwards she knew she would need far more determination and guts than she possessed. How could she do anything other than fall? She had never liked heights; she didn't trust her balance. Who would help her?

Subsumed once more in her own misery, rather as she had been after killing Tomas Brodinski, Josie hardly noticed the kind and caring professionals gently guiding her over the crevasse and onto the safer foothills of the mountain. Nor, initially, did she realise how much the touching concern of her friends helped her to build up a sense of self-worth.

It was her thirty-third birthday at the end of February. When she looked at the birthday cards pinned to the noticeboard in her room she realised with surprise that she had received more than she had had since she was a child. Most of them were hand-made, some of them were illiterate, but all of them sent love and best wishes from the other inmates. Amy had drawn a picture of a sunflower with a sombrero perched on its head and the message 'the sun is always shining somewhere if you look for it'. Joyce had pasted a picture of a blackbird onto yellow card and her message read 'dear Jo keep on singing, love Joyce xxxxxx' (except she had left the first 'n' out so it read siging, which made Josie smile). Sharon had given her a chocolate bar and a card with a picture of a furry rabbit; she had written 'keep going kiddo'. There were lots of others too, some from girls she hardly knew; they made her feel special. The chaplain called on her and said happy birthday and that she hoped Josie would be back in the choir on Sunday because they were missing her. Her personal officer put her head round the door at break-time and said she hoped Josie would have a nice day. At supper her table sang Happy Birthday and were so rowdy that the officers on duty had to come over and suggest, pleasantly, that a bit less noise would be a good idea. All in all the day ended with her feeling much happier than she had for some weeks.

Not long after her birthday she made the monumental decision to sell her house. It was a snap decision that was most unlike her. The therapy session that day had been all about moving on, making plans for the future and putting strategies into place to avoid a repetition of past behaviour. After weeks in denial she was beginning to understand her own situation; at last she could see more clearly how she had been manipulated into thinking she had been in a loving relationship.

Despite her very considerable reservations she had also been persuaded to join a group discussion. It had been a revelation. She had heard the stories of other prisoners. What she herself had been through was as nothing compared to most of them: abusive partners, fathers, 'uncles'; many of the women controlled to such an extent that they were not free to live their lives in any meaningful way. Josie had no idea that these things happened. She was appalled at the suffering of the women and also of their many children. It was astonishing, though, that these women were able to laugh about their experiences and engage in role play that had them falling around in fits of laughter.

To her surprise she had found that she no longer minded the other prisoners knowing her own past history. This new-found sisterhood was empowering; she felt a weight falling from her as she recognised the start of her own recovery.

She realised with startling clarity that selling her house was an obvious thing to do. It would remove at a stroke so many of the memories that were now increasingly painful. She could obliterate all practical reminders of her father; all his furniture, books, garden tools could be got rid of. She could start again, really start again, and living somewhere new would be a first step.

Later that day she used her phone card and rang David Owens, asking him to put her house on the market as soon as possible.

Chapter 33

SUPPER WAS OVER in the Pearson household. Di and Peter's younger son, Dan, had drifted upstairs in a desultory way to do his homework. There had been the usual bargaining about being let off the table clearing, dishwasher loading and breakfast laying in return for being in bed by ten o'clock without his iPhone and having done the requisite two hours of maths revision – and having had a shower.

Di sank wearily back into her chair; she ran her hands through her short dark hair and then cupped her chin in her hands, elbows on the table, and looked at Peter sitting opposite.

'Your turn to do battle tomorrow evening, don't you think?' she raised an eyebrow at him. 'Why is Dan so much worse than Edward was?' referring to their elder son who was now satisfactorily at university.

'Dunno.' Peter had got home late from work and had arrived in the middle of the argument. 'D'you want coffee?' He got up to make it.

'Please. I meant to say this morning that I think I had better go and see Josie again – at the end of next week probably.' Di didn't sound enthusiastic.

'Why?' Peter looked in the fridge for a carton of milk.

'I had said I would visit again in January and then of course I didn't as we had the 'flu; and now we're into March and I'm feeling guilty.'

'She'll be out soon, won't she?' Peter passed her a mug.

'Thanks. May, I think, near the beginning, so there's a bit of a way to go still.'

'Up to you, I guess, if you think it's worthwhile.'

'Well, at least I give her a link with the outside world. I don't think she has many of them.' Di sipped her coffee contemplatively.

'That reminds me.' Peter put his mug down and wiped his mouth with the back of his hand. 'I was driving down Woodfield Road a few days ago and I noticed that Josie's house was up for sale.'

'You can't be right?' Di looked puzzled.

'Isn't it the one more or less opposite old Vinnie Jones?'

'Yes; but you can't be right. Did you see who the estate agent was?'

'One of the local ones, I think.'

Di reached for her phone. 'I'll check Rightmove and see if it's there.' She looked intently at the screen for a few moments. 'It looks as if you're right. That's hers. But why on earth would she sell?'

'Perhaps she doesn't want to come back to Northwood when she comes out.'

'Why ever not? She seemed so content in that house, just her and her Dad. And after he died she didn't want to move then. Why now?'

'New start, new place, maybe?'

'I'll find out next week, then.' Di drained her mug and got up from the table. 'Seems a pretty big decision to have taken.'

Chapter 34

WHEN THE NEW YEAR had turned Josie was initially disappointed not to hear from Di. She had been looking forward to seeing her again and finding out what was going on in Northwood. Then, as her own situation had become so fraught, she had been glad not to have to explain or justify to someone on the outside what was going on in her own life. She had concentrated all her energies on her immediate predicament; it was therefore with surprise that she learned from a brief letter that Di was coming to see her on a Saturday in early March.

They met, as before, in the visits centre where Di was sitting waiting. She saw Josie come in through the door with a group of other women, escorted by officers. Di watched her cross the room: she looked different somehow; her hair was cut short into a bob and she was wearing a navy jersey over a white shirt with black trousers, the old white trainers replaced with new blue ones. She moved more purposefully, Di thought, as if she knew what she was doing and was confident doing it. She was exchanging banter with one of the other women and both of them were laughing as they parted company.

'See yer, Jo.' The other woman said as she moved away.

Di got up and kissed Josie on both cheeks. 'You're looking well.' She said as they sat down.

'Thank you.' Josie smiled. 'I was sorry to hear you had the 'flu; are you all right now?'

'Fine, thanks. Did it find its way in here, too?'

'Not really; quite a few girls had colds and sore throats but it wasn't a 'flu epidemic as such, thank goodness.'

They talked for some minutes about Northwood and about prison life and Di was struck by Josie's manner. She would almost call it self-assured. Remarkably different from the shy, diffident girl she had worked with in the wardrobe room last summer.

Di had intended to mention the sale of Josie's house but before she had made up her mind about it Josie raised the subject.

'I daresay you've seen the 'for sale' sign outside my house, haven't you?' she asked.

Di nodded. 'Yes, Peter saw it about two weeks ago.' She waited for Josie to enlarge.

'You must have thought I was mad or that I was being kept in a lot longer than expected?' Josie was smiling.

Di laughed. 'We were certainly surprised. Does it mean you are not coming back to Northwood, then, when you come out?'

'Not necessarily. The house is too big for me, for one thing, and I won't be working in the Planning Office either, so I can be more flexible over where I live. But the main reason is that I want to make a fresh start. Being in here has made me look at my life rather differently and I think I'd like to make a proper break from the old Josie, if I can.' She looked at Di.

'Good for you.' Di was impressed; she had also noticed that the other prisoner had called Josie 'Jo'. 'Where might you go and have you got another job lined up as well?'

'I'm not sure yet. I've been doing a horticultural diploma whilst I've been inside. I'm hoping to complete it – and pass it – before I come out. Have you heard of a new nursery called Highfields? It's about five miles west of Northwood?'

Di shook her head.

'Well,' Josie went on, 'they've not been open long and are looking for staff. They specialise in hardy perennials. My supervisor, Mr P, knows one of the owners and I am to have an interview there next month. I may not get the job, of course, they may not like employing an ex-offender but it's worth a try and if I don't there are other places not too far away. So I hope to go on living in Northwood, and maybe buy a flat.' She grinned at Di. 'Did you say last time you came that Mike's flat was empty?'

Di smiled then burst out laughing, causing the group at the next table to stop talking and the officers nearby to look up with surprise at the noise.

'Actually,' Josie went on, 'you could help by telling me what's on the market locally, if you wouldn't mind. I can't access the internet in here and local newspapers would be out of date by the time I saw them, even if I could get hold of them. Would you have time to send me details of anything suitable?'

'Of course I will. I'll have a look to see what the estate agents have got on their books and let you know.'

'Thanks, that would be great.'

They discussed possible flats in Northwood and Josie told Di what she would ideally like to buy. She said that David Owens had told her that there had already been some interest in her old house but that it was unlikely it would be sold before she came out, certainly not completed. She didn't tell Di the real reason why she never wanted to go back there again.

Chapter 35

'Jo, how many boyfriends 'ave you 'ad?'

Josie and Joyce were sitting after work in a corner of the library reading an old copy of *Today* magazine. At least Joyce was supposed to be doing the reading. She had managed reasonably well but had become distracted by photographs of some of her favourite female celebrities hanging on the arms of assorted male escorts. There had been much oohing and aahing at the clothes of the women and the desirability of the favoured men.

'Nobody serious,' Josie replied.

'Go on, yer must 'ave.'

'Not really.'

'So how many 'ave yer gone to bed with, then?'

'None.' Josie wondered where this was going. She turned a page of the magazine hoping to deflect Joyce from further enquiries.

There was a pause as Joyce peered up at Josie again.

'That'll be 'cos of your Dad, then.' This was a statement.

'Perhaps.'

'What'll yer do when yer get out, about boyfriends I mean?'

'Nothing.'

'That'd be a waste; yer'll have to make an effort, yer know. Yer could be pretty if yer did yer hair proper and used make-up.' Joyce was quite indignant at the thought of Josie living a boyfriend-free existence. It didn't make sense to her.

'I'll see. Now try reading this page.' She angled the new page towards Joyce.

But Joyce was intent on her next thought.

'What'll I do when yer gone, then? Who's goin' to help me learn to read?'

'You're getting on fine, you won't need anyone to help you in a week or two and I'm here for another six weeks, anyway.'

'I'll miss yer badly, Jo, when yer gone.' Joyce looked dejected.

'I shall miss you, too.' Josie replied and realised that she meant it. 'We can always write to each other, you know. It'd be good practice, wouldn't it?'

'I s'pose.' Joyce looked more cheerful. 'Will yer come and visit me?'

'I'm not allowed to drive for ages, and I've sold my car anyway.'

'I remember yer told me.' Joyce's smile disappeared.

'Maybe you should ask for a transfer nearer home?' Josie put the magazine down. She looked round to see if the librarian was watching them as chatting wasn't permitted in the library, but she was relieved to see her behind the counter dealing with several other women.

'There isn't anywhere nearer to Aberystwyth,' Joyce said. 'D'yer think I should go back there when I'm let out? I mean to me Mam an' all? The thinking skills people said I should start again, but where would I go? I don' want to live in a hostel. What could I do, anyway?'

'What about your aunt who came to see you just after Christmas, Auntie Beryl, didn't you say? Couldn't you go to her?'

'She's nice, is Auntie Beryl. I wouldn't mind goin' there, and she did say I could, if I wanted, so long as I behaved meself.'

'Well, then, where does she live?'

'Near Wrexham. I stayed with her once when Mam was havin' trouble with one of 'er chaps and wanted me gone. It was okay.' Joyce frowned as she weighed up the possibility of going to Wrexham. She sighed. 'But then there's Wayne. How do I keep him away when he gets out?'

'That's not going to be for ages, you know that. You need to talk to Mr Salisbury at your next meeting, don't you think? You said he was pleased about you coming off Methadone, and that he'd help you find somewhere new to go to so you don't relapse. When you've got your English and Maths you can get a job in here; that'll help you decide what to do next. It'll be all right, you'll see.' Josie stood up; the library lady was approaching and she knew it was time they went back to Beech House.

'That's an awful lot of stuff to do without yer helpin' me.' Joyce's thin shoulders sagged.

'You can do it.' Josie was surprised at her own optimism and assertiveness.

Chapter 36

'JO, ARE YOU READY? It's time we left.'

'Just coming.' Josie patted her lips with a tissue to remove excess lipstick. She gave a quick glance in the mirror before picking up her handbag and anorak. It was strange to be wearing lipstick again and she had put on her smarter trousers with proper shoes, not trainers. Waiting for her in the passage was her personal officer, Miss Richards, who was driving her to Highfields Nursery for a job interview.

'You okay? You look neat and tidy.' Jenny Richards nodded approvingly.

'Yes, thank you,' Josie replied as they made their way to the gatehouse.

Many times in the last five months Josie had passed the gatehouse and watched staff and visitors coming and going. It had been hard seeing them getting into their cars and driving out onto the main road and away at the end of a day when she was forced to stay behind the wire fence. They took their freedom for granted, she supposed, and seemingly gave no more thought to the prison inmates as they left for home in their Toyotas and Vauxhalls. But now it was her turn to go out and even though she knew she would be returning in a few hours it still seemed to be a monumental occasion. She watched Miss Richards hand in her keys and sign both of them out and then as they waited by the double gates she heard the decisive click as the lock was remotely operated and first one huge gate was opened and then when that had closed behind them she heard the second click indicating the lock was released on the second gate. There was a car waiting for them close to the gates and another officer handed Miss Richards the keys and checked that she knew where she was going. Josie got into the front passenger seat and fastened her seatbelt. There were five hours of freedom ahead and she felt excited.

They chatted companionably as the car sped through the Midlands countryside. We could just be two friends out for a ride on a pleasant spring day, Josie thought. Miss Richards wasn't wearing her uniform so no one would know they were prisoner and guard. It was strange seeing early signs of spring; the daffodils were out in gardens along the road, the verges had turned green again as the weather had improved and reduced the splattering of muddy water from the traffic. There was some early blossom showing, almond possibly, and just the hint here and there of green in the hawthorn hedges. The fruit trees were starting to break into blossom behind the garden workshops in the prison and there were masses of daffodils cheering up the paths on the way to the dining room but somehow seeing it on the outside was different. Josie sat back in her seat and temporarily forgot about her nervousness over the impending job interview as she drank in the unaccustomed scenery. Seeing miles and miles of countryside without looking at it through wire-mesh fencing was liberating.

An hour and a half later they were approaching Northwood.

'Do we pass your house, Jo?' Jenny Richards asked as she negotiated a roundabout with a sign saying Northwood two miles.

'No, it's just off the main road. If we've time on the way home could you possibly drive that way, do you think?'

'Let's see when we leave the nursery. We'll need to stop somewhere for a coffee and sandwich, either before or after Northwood, so it'll depend a bit on that. I wouldn't be able to let you out to look, you know.'

'I know, but the house is up for sale and I would like to see the sign, if you didn't mind.'

'I'll see. Now let's just run through some of the questions you might be asked by Mr Simonds – that's his name isn't it?'

Miss Richards rehearsed Josie's answers for the next few miles until she had to concentrate on finding the side road to the nursery. They turned off the main road and the lane wound uphill for a mile or so through fields dotted with sheep and newborn lambs enjoying the spring sunshine. Josie began to feel nervous again; her stomach was churning as they neared their destination. Serious doubts about her qualifications for the job and her ability to do it resurfaced. She was sure that Mr Simonds wouldn't want an ex-offender working for him. She was sure he would think she would be a bad influence on other workers. Her apprehension grew as they turned into the car park. Feelings of panic rose in her and she gripped her seat. Jenny Richards eased the car into a space between two others and turned to Josie. She put her hand on Josie's arm.

'Take a few deep breaths before you get out. You're going to be fine. He can't eat you, you know!'

Josie looked at her gratefully and breathed deeply. The panic slowly subsided.

'Go on, then, remember eye contact and don't be afraid to say if you don't know the answer or understand the question. Good luck.' Jenny smiled encouragingly.

'Thanks.'

In the event she was pleasantly surprised. It was all rather laid back, nothing formal at all. Mr Simonds had welcomed her warmly, he had been in one of the polytunnels when she arrived and another, younger man had directed her to find him. Miss Richards had stayed in the car.

He hadn't even shaken hands with her as his were covered with a mixture of compost and horticultural sand.

'Hi there,' he had said, raising a dirty hand in greeting when she entered the polytunnel. He gestured at some hardy fuchsias waiting to be repotted. 'I'm afraid I need to get these finished this morning, Josephine, as we've got an order going out tomorrow that'll need my attention all afternoon. Do you mind helping? Pour yourself a coffee.' He indicated a thermos on the bench beside him. 'Milk's in the carton, d'you want sugar?'

She shook her head, poured coffee into a plastic cup and added milk.

'Here you go,' he said and pushed some empty flowerpots over to her. 'Fill them about half full before you put the plants in and firm them well. What do you like being called? Josephine, Jo, Josie?' He raised an eyebrow at her in a friendly way.

'Jo is fine, thank you.'

'Right, Jo, I'm Paul and we'll chat as we work, if that's okay. Tony said you were a good timekeeper, a hard worker and showed a real interest in plants. That true?'

'I hope so,' Josie replied shyly, guessing that Tony was her supervisor, Mr P. She hadn't known his first name.

'That's a good start anyway.'

He did most of the talking for the next hour or so telling her how he had set up the nursery and what his ideas were for its expansion, which was why he needed more staff. Josie said very little to start with but knew that she was being ever so gently interviewed as they worked together. It wasn't an unpleasant feeling. Paul pulled her leg several times when she told him she had worked for some years in the local planning office. He seemed surprised and pleased when she told him that she had helped to set up the council's new planning website a year ago.

'That's great; I am intending to sell most of our stuff online in the near future.' He stopped working for a moment and leaned on the bench looking at her. 'It would be a huge help if you understand all the implications as I'm rather a novice with IT, I'm afraid.'

Nor did he seem to mind at all about her prison sentence, to Josie's huge relief.

'Your private life is your own concern,' he had said. 'I want my staff to be pleasant and professional, to get on with each other and to get the work done without moaning – even if the weather is awful.' He laughed. 'It can be awful up here, I can tell you.'

She asked him about transport to work, if she was offered the job.

'Ah yes, you're disqualified, aren't you?'

She nodded without looking at him.

'Shouldn't be a problem. My younger brother, Ian, he showed you in here when you arrived, he manages the sales side of the business. He lives just west of Northwood and could probably give you a lift most days; you could cycle to his house. Do you have a bike?'

'No, but I was thinking of getting one,' Josie said.

'Good, but there's also a regular bus service along the

main road; you'd have to walk the mile or so up here from the bottom of the hill, but it only takes about fifteen minutes.'

They finished potting the fuchsias.

'Thanks, that's a job well done.' He wiped his hands on his dungarees.

'You'll need a wash before you drive back. There's a cloakroom at the far end of that brick building.' He gestured out of the polytunnel door, 'I'll see you in a minute by your car.'

She walked through the sales area where plants, neatly potted, labelled and priced, were ranged alphabetically in timber-edged beds. She could see new shoots poking up through the compost and new leaves tentatively uncurling, reaching for the spring sunshine. The sales office was to the side where Ian, she supposed, was working, as well as several other people whom she hadn't met.

'Will he offer me the job? Or will he say I'm not suitable, or will I have to wait to find out?' As she washed her hands and tidied herself as best she could she decided that she very much wanted to be offered the job. She liked Paul. She had felt totally comfortable working alongside him. He was the first man she had had contact with since the evening with Mike, apart from David Owens and the prison staff, but it had been fine and there were no panicky feelings even when his arm unintentionally brushed against hers as he reached for a flower pot. She liked the way the nursery was set up too; it seemed organised and efficient. Paul's plans for the future were interesting and she thought she would like to be part of them.

As she left the washroom she paused and looked across the valley towards the Welsh hills. To her left and right were shelter belts of beech trees, moderating the winds from the south-west and north, the nursery snugly tucked in-between the trees. Ahead, to the west, were the blue misty outlines of hills, rising higher and higher towards Snowdon, she guessed. She stood for a moment savouring the view and feeling the wind blowing through her hair. After the flat Midlands countryside of Edgehill it was exhilarating to be up here on the Welsh borders. She took a deep breath.

'This is freedom.'

Josie wasn't sure if she had said the words out loud or not, but she had a sudden yearning to shout and hear her words tossed into the wind and blown beyond reach, dissipating through the white breeze-blown clouds.

'I will be free.'

In her imagination she could hear echoes rebounding across the valley telling the grazing sheep and cattle that something marvellous was about to happen. For nearly six months she had been constrained: she had got up in the morning and gone to bed at night when ordered. She had no say in what she ate or where she went or what she did. Her horizons had been the wire fence; her aspirations had been to get through each day without conflict. Now she had a chance to start again.

'I will not be defined by my father's abuse. I will get a new job; if not this one then there will be another somewhere. I will travel; I will visit Sophia and Mrs Brodinski and see if I can help them; I will try and help Joyce; I will carry on singing; I will make new friends; I will be Jo not Josie.'

As she stood looking across the valley she knew she was on the threshold of something. She wasn't sure what, but she knew it would be good. Then she remembered that Paul and Jenny would be waiting for her.

'Please let him say yes. Oh please.'

As she returned to the car she could see Paul chatting with Jenny Richards, both of them leaning in a relaxed fashion against the passenger doors.

'Well,' he said, smiling at her as she approached 'if you're happy to accept low pay and lots of bad weather I should like to offer you the job.' He stood upright and held out his now clean right hand.

Josie couldn't disguise her delight; she blushed with pleasure and her smile felt a mile wide, stretching her face in an unfamiliar way. She hadn't done much smiling since last July.

'Oh.' She grasped his hand. 'Thank you so much. I'll really do my best.' She looked at Jenny who was also smiling broadly.

They discussed a few details about contracts and starting dates and then Jenny said they must be on their way if Paul didn't need to talk to Jo about anything else.

He said 'No, that's fine, and I'll be in touch via Tony in the next day or two. Good bye, Jo, it's been good to meet you and I'll see you again soon.' He stood back from the car as Jenny reversed out and then waved them off, his tall, angular figure silhouetted against the sky.

Chapter 37

WELL, JO,' Sadie Harrison said cheerfully. 'Nearly there; release date imminent and you've got yourself a job, I see.' She was looking at a copy of a letter from Paul Simonds outlining terms and conditions of Josie's employment with Highfields Nursery.

Josie nodded; her eyes were bright and she looked more relaxed than Sadie had ever seen her.

'Good girl,' Sadie went on. 'I'm really pleased for you; now we just need to tidy up odds and ends of your sentence plan and look at what you need to do when you are released to ensure you don't darken our doorstep again at Edgehill.'

'I won't be back.'

'I should hope not! There's one other thing before we carry on: I have a letter from Sophia Brodinski in reply to yours. I wasn't expecting to hear from her or her mother again but you obviously made an impression when you wrote and it seems she would like to keep in touch with you. I'm not quite sure why.' She rummaged on her desk and then passed a sheet of white paper over to Josie. 'Maybe the best thing is for you to decide what you want to do about corresponding and let her know directly.'

Josie took the paper and glanced at it. 'It's rather a coincidence that she's written as I have been thinking a lot about them recently.' She paused and looked apprehensively at Sadie. 'I wondered if I couldn't now consider making some sort of recompense to them.'

'So, what do you have in mind?' Sadie was interested.

'Well, I know my car insurance company has paid them quite a bit but maybe I could send money directly to Sophia to help with her university fees. Tomas was doing that, you see, and they must miss the money badly.'

'Interesting idea but can you afford to do it?'

'I heard from my solicitor last week that someone has put in quite a good offer on my house, which he wants me to accept. The flat I hope to buy is a lot less so I could afford to give some away. I would like to do that if it's possible.' She looked enquiringly at Sadie.

Sadie nodded slowly as she thought about the proposal. 'It's not something the prison service could get involved in but I would talk it through with your solicitor when you get out and see how he thinks it could be arranged. It would seem to me to be a very good thing to do.' She looked impressed.

They talked some more about Josie's continuing rehabilitation, Sadie reiterating her belief that Josie was more than ready to reintegrate into society without any further need of counselling.

'You have clearly come to terms with what happened,' she said. 'I have had the final report from your abuse counsellor and it seems to me that you should now be able to form normal friendships without your previous feelings of insecurity and panic reasserting themselves, if you wanted to do so. Obviously it will take time to readjust, but you've come a long way.'

'I suppose so. I have made proper friends with some of the girls in here which is a start, I guess.' Josie said slowly. 'But it will be different outside, won't it?'

'Perhaps; you must take it slowly at first. Best not jump head first into any relationship,' Sadie smiled. 'You should stop and look at yourself, you know; you are so much more confident now; you walk with your head up, literally and metaphorically; you've found yourself a job – all right (as Josie demurred) – I know Mr P laid the groundwork, forgive the pun, but you obviously presented well at interview. You got the job on merit, didn't you?'

'Maybe.' Josie was smiling too.

'You've also made a difference to the other women here in Edgehill, so give yourself a break. Go out and start to enjoy life and make up for what you missed during all those years. You know where the help is if you need it.' Sadie stood up and held out her hand. 'Best of luck, Jo, it's been a pleasure working with you.'

Josie shook her hand warmly. 'Thank you for helping me to believe in myself. I couldn't have done it without you and the counselling team. I'm really grateful.' She paused. 'Perhaps getting a prison sentence was almost a godsend.' She smiled ruefully.

'That's a bit dramatic, but there may be a whisker of truth in it – desperate remedies and all that.' Sadie laughed and crossed to the door and opened it. Josie started to leave then turned to thank Sadie again.

Sadie put her hand up indicating that enough had been said.

'Off you go now and good luck.'

Chapter 38

JOSIE HAD ONE MORE DAY of work to do in the gardens before her release from prison. It was the beginning of May and there was a spring-like bustle in the gardening office with Mr P handing out secateurs and shears whilst exhorting everyone to get a move on as he needed at least a dozen different jobs completed by lunchtime and there were not enough girls to do them.

'You can shift the new delivery of compost into the far polytunnel,' he said to two of the women. Then I shall want you on the mowers if the dew has dried off. You three,' he turned to another group, 'get yourselves down to the front offices and get the grass edges trimmed and tidied up; take the wheelbarrow and a broom with you.' He turned to the women who had been given secateurs 'we didn't finish tidying the shrubs by the gym last month. Give the laurels a haircut and get all the old leaves swept up from underneath. You'll need a wheelbarrow and a rake too.'

Only Josie and Amy were left awaiting instructions. 'I want you two to rake over the plot for the peas and beans,' he said to them. 'Take out as many stones as you can and then we can sow the second lot of peas in situ this afternoon if you get a move on and maybe get the main crop potatoes into the ground as well, in the far plot that we cleared last week. I've got the pea seeds over here and the potatoes are in a box behind my desk. Off you go.'

'You know its Jo's last day, Mr P?' Amy turned by the door and looked back at him enquiringly.

'Yes, indeed I do. And without Jo I shall expect you to be working twice as hard next week, young lady!'

'No chance, man,' Amy retorted gaily, her gold hoop earrings twinkling in the sun as she flounced out of the door.

'Don't leave this afternoon without seeing me, please Jo,' Mr P called as Josie made to follow Amy.

Josie nodded and hurried out.

She caught up with Amy by the vegetable plot. They had given it a rough digging over a few days ago and it wasn't going to require too much hard work to get it ready for planting the peas and beans. Amy, however, beckoned Josie over to where she was waiting, out of sight of Mr P in his office.

'I got somethin' for yous, Jo,' she said conspiratorially, her hand in her overalls pocket. 'Come over 'ere.'

Josie looked over her shoulder, following Amy's glance towards the office. No one was in sight so she moved closer.

''S okay,' Amy said quietly, 'he's goin' to be busy all mornin' doin' 'is stats, 'e said.'

'What is it?' Josie was puzzled.

'See, I got it for yous; the chaplain helped. D'yer like it then?' She thrust a small package wrapped in a tissue into Josie's hand.

Josie unwrapped the tissue carefully and found she was holding a silver-coloured pendant on a chain. The pendant had a woman's figure on it; she had her hand extended as if she was giving something away.

'It's lovely,' she said cautiously. 'Who's the lady?'

'It's Saint Dorothy,' Amy said proudly, 'she's the patron saint of gardeners. She was a martyr hundreds of years ago, she was tortured an' put on the rack.' Amy was enjoying the gruesome details. 'I reckon she'll look after yous.'

'Oh, thank you so much, Amy, I'll wear it now.' She fastened the clasp round her neck and positioned the pendant on top of her work overalls so that Amy could see it. 'I'm sure she'll look after me. Do you know when her saint's day is?'

'Yeah, February the sixth; yer'll have to say a prayer to her next year.'

'I must try and remember. Otherwise I might have bad luck, don't you think?'

Josie gave Amy a hug, then turned away to pick up her rake hoping Amy hadn't seen the tears welling up. She sniffed and quickly wiped her eyes with the back of her hand before launching into 'Amazing Grace', which was one of Amy's favourite songs.

Saying goodbye to Mr P hadn't been much easier either. He had been so kind and helpful and without him pulling strings she knew she wouldn't have had an interview, let alone been offered the job by Paul Simonds.

She tried to thank him but he laughed and said she'd have managed fine with or without his help and the best thanks he could have would be for him to hear she had been made a partner in the business in a couple of years' time.

'You can do it, you know, Jo. Carry on with your studying and get Paul to release you for college, and then with a few certificates and your IT skills you'll be an invaluable asset to him. You see if I'm not right.'

They shook hands and he patted her on the back. 'Good luck, girl,' he said. 'We'll miss you.'

She walked slowly back to Beech House from the gardening office. She knew every inch of the way. She passed the forsythia bushes outside the gymnasium on her left;

they had been a glorious golden yellow in March and then she and Amy had pruned them back only a week or two ago. They had found an old nest in the tangled branches and Josie had wondered if it had belonged to her friend the blackbird, though he and his mate had a new nest in the ivy on the wall of the chapel. Recently she had seen them coming and going with worms from the newly dug vegetable patches and crumbs of bread that the women had put out on the grass and she guessed their eggs had hatched. She felt sad that she wouldn't see the fledglings leave the nest.

Further along the path she passed the spot where she had been ambushed by Noreen. The memories of being a hostage were ones that she would rather forget and yet she realised that the event had triggered something subconsciously within her that then led to the confession to Sadie Harrison about her father. Maybe she had something to thank Noreen for after all.

Briefly she thought about her parents. It had been so painful to face up to what had happened and to try and understand it. She was still perplexed about her mother: had she known what was going on? Was her supposed ill health a cover-up and an escape from something she couldn't deal with? But why not protect her only child? Surely that's what mothers did?

Josie pushed the unwelcome thoughts away. She had learned so much in the last six months and in the counselling sessions in particular; she had now regained control of her life. It was possible to accept the fact that she would never know the reasons for the abuse but also to know that it didn't matter any more. She had a new life ahead from tomorrow and it was going to be better than the old one.

She was sure of that. She turned onto the path leading to Beech House and pushed open the bashed-up swing doors; tomorrow she would go out of these familiar doors for the last time; she would be leaving prison – for good.

Saying goodbye to her friends in Beech House was even more difficult than saying goodbye to Mr P and Amy. After evening lock-up a group of them congregated in the association room and when Josie arrived, dragged there by Joyce, they sang 'For She's a Jolly Good Fellow' and gave her good luck cards and a variety of mementoes. Josie was half-expecting a bit of a fuss to be made and had bought a box of chocolates to share with them all.

The evening became rather emotional and after an hour or so Josie excused herself on the grounds of needing to finish packing up her things and went back to her room. She didn't want to break down in front of the others. Joyce insisted on coming too; she was very upset.

'What'll I do without you, Jo?' she kept saying. Josie, having reiterated her previous advice, tried to find something for Joyce to do to stop her from bursting into tears and starting her off too.

'Here, write down the names of all the Beech House girls for me, so that I don't forget anyone.' She handed Joyce an old exercise book and a pen. Joyce was kept busy for some time with the spelling of the names, and Josie managed to finish her packing more or less uninterrupted.

'Yer'll write to me, Jo, won't yer?' Joyce looked more woebegone than ever. She gave the exercise book back to Josie.

'Yes, of course I will. You know I will, and we'll meet up when you get out.' She got up from the floor where she had been kneeling whilst she put her last things into a holdall. 'Now, let's make a cup of tea and then I must have a shower. I'll bang on your door in the morning and we can say a proper goodbye then. Come on now, go and fetch your mug.'

Chapter 39

B Y MID-MAY the Northwood Amateur Operatic Society was well into rehearsals for its next summer production. It had been decided the previous autumn that another Gilbert and Sullivan opera would please the local community – there had been so many compliments about *The Mikado* that striking whilst the iron was hot, as the producer put it, would be a good idea. *Trial by Jury* had been agreed after a committee vote.

The cast had congregated as usual in the village hall for the evening's rehearsal. Some people were standing on the stage and others were perched on chairs and tables or leaning against the side walls whilst they waited for the producer to give them his notes before the rehearsal started.

The producer moved rather self-importantly to the centre of the hall and cleared his throat noisily whilst waving his notes in the air to get everyone's attention. With the palm of his other hand he self-consciously smoothed down his comb-over.

'Let's have a bit of hush for a moment. Thank you, thank you,' he beamed as silence fell. 'Just before I give you the notes from our last rehearsal I have some really good news.' He cleared his throat again. 'I am truly delighted, and I know you will be too, to welcome back an old member of our society – at least she isn't old, that's quite inaccurate – how rude of me --but she is a past member and I'm so pleased she's back with us, and will be helping Di again with the costumes this season. You never know, we might just persuade her to tread the boards too. Now that would be good!' He looked over to the side of the hall. 'Please give a big welcome back to Josie Anderson.' He tucked his notes under his arm and led the clapping enthusiastically.

Everyone looked pleased and as the clapping died away Di gave Josie a small shove.

'You'd better say something,' she whispered.

Josie stepped forward, her hand instinctively touching the Saint Dorothy pendant round her neck. 'Thank you very much, it's kind of you to welcome me.' She nodded her thanks at the producer. 'It's good to be here and lovely to see you all. Just one thing, though, I'm Jo now; my name is Jo.'